She spun around to see Chase Miller looki

"Yeah, Mia—look, I know we haven't really talked before, but this is kind of important."

"Is this about the tutoring? Because I told Mr. Haves that those last two tests were just accidents and I'm fine."

"That's not why I'm here. Actually, it's about the spell you did yesterday."

"What?" Mia yelped as she glanced around. "O-of course I didn't do a spell. W-why would you even say something like that?"

"Because I know a spell was done at Newbury High at the exact time I saw you behind the bleachers at the senior awards assembly yesterday," he said, and Mia let out a groan.

"Look, all I need is the incantation you used."

"Why? So you can tell the whole school I did a love spell? Besides, it wasn't *really* a love spell, because that would imply Rob didn't like me and he did—er, does."

"Okay, the thing is, it doesn't really matter what sort of spell you think you did, because—"

"It might not matter to you, but it matters to me." Mia bristled as she thought about her adorable dress that was hanging in her closet in preparation for Friday night.

"Sorry, I just meant that we have a bigger problem on our hands. What you actually did was an ancient ritual called *Viral Zombaticus.*"

"You're still not making any sense."

"I'm not doing a very good job of this," he admitted as he took a deep breath. "But what I'm trying to say is that when you did that spell yesterday, you inadvertently turned everyone who was at the assembly into flesh-eating zombies."

OTHER BOOKS YOU MAY ENJOY

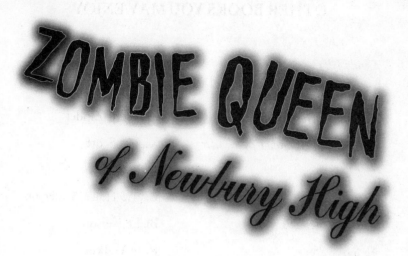

ZOMBIE QUEEN
of Newbury High

Amanda
Ashby

speak
An Imprint of Penguin Group (USA) Inc.

SPEAK
Published by the Penguin Group
Penguin Group (USA) Inc., 345 Hudson Street, New York, New York 10014, U.S.A.
Penguin Group (Canada), 90 Eglinton Avenue East, Suite 700, Toronto, Ontario, Canada M4P 2Y3
(a division of Pearson Penguin Canada Inc.)
Penguin Books Ltd, 80 Strand, London WC2R 0RL, England
Penguin Ireland, 25 St Stephen's Green, Dublin 2, Ireland (a division of Penguin Books Ltd)
Penguin Group (Australia), 250 Camberwell Road, Camberwell, Victoria 3124, Australia
(a division of Pearson Australia Group Pty Ltd)
Penguin Books India Pvt Ltd, 11 Community Centre, Panchsheel Park, New Delhi - 110 017, India
Penguin Group (NZ), 67 Apollo Drive, Rosedale, North Shore 0632, New Zealand
(a division of Pearson New Zealand Ltd)
Penguin Books (South Africa) (Pty) Ltd, 24 Sturdee Avenue,
Rosebank, Johannesburg 2196, South Africa

Registered Offices: Penguin Books Ltd, 80 Strand, London WC2R 0RL, England

Published by Speak, an imprint of Penguin Group (USA) Inc., 2008

3 4 5 6 7 8 9 10

Copyright ©Amanda Ashby, 2009
All rights reserved

LIBRARY OF CONGRESS CATALOGING-IN PUBLICATION DATA
Ashby, Amanda.
Zombie Queen of Newbury High / by Amanda Ashby.
p. cm.
Summary: While trying to cast a love spell on her date on the eve of the senior prom,
Mia inadvertently infects her entire high school class with a virus
that will turn them all into zombies.

ISBN: 978-0-14-241256-5 (pbk. : alk. paper)
[1. Zombies—Fiction. 2. Proms—Fiction. 3. Blessing and cursing—Fiction.
4. High School—Fiction. 5. Schools—Fiction.]
I. Title.
PZ7.A7993Zom 2009
[Fic]—dc22 2008041035

Speak ISBN 978-0-14-241256-5

Printed in the United States of America

To Barry, Molly, and Arthur. Forever and always.

Acknowledgments

Before I started writing this book, it was fair to say that my critique partners, Christina Phillips, Pat Posner, and Sara Hantz, weren't exactly zombie fans. I'm so grateful that they let me draw them over to the dark side. If they can take on the living dead, I think they can take on just about anything.

To my fabulous agent, Jenny Bent, who loved the idea of this book right from the start. Thank you, thank you, thank you.

To my amazing editor, Karen Chaplin, for working so hard to find the real story. And to everyone else at Puffin for doing what you all do so well. I feel so lucky to be allowed to come along for the ride.

To my mother, Pam, I have no idea how you're going to convince your book group to read this one! To Marjory Holt and all my other in-laws in Liverpool, thank you for making me feel like an honorary scouser. As for my friends and family scattered around the world, yes I know I forgot to send Christmas cards last year, but look what I was busy doing. Forgive me?

I'd also like to say thank you to all the cool new cyber buddies I've met since I went online to promote my last book. You guys have truly made me feel like an honest-to-goodness author girl. Thank you. (Oh, and buy this book as well, will you!)

To my children, Molly and Arthur, for thinking it's completely normal to have a mother who makes them walk like zombies so she can take notes. And finally, to my husband, Barry, for putting up with my David Boreanaz obsession and getting me addicted to Hammer Films all those years ago. I blame you entirely!

one

$\mathcal{M}$ia Everett was doomed. It was a fact she had known ever since Rob Ziggerman walked into biology class half an hour earlier. Instead of sitting next to her, as had been his habit for the last month, he'd made a beeline for Samantha Griffin. All of which meant the rumors must be true.

"How can this be happening?" she demanded in a low voice as she turned to Candice, who was carefully inspecting the skin of her elbow by poking it with a pencil.

"I have no idea." Her friend shook her shoulder-length red hair in disgust as she offered up her arm for inspection. "I'm only seventeen. It hardly seems fair, but it's definitely leprosy. No doubt about it. See the way the skin is falling away like that? Textbook case."

"Candice, I'm not talking about you, I'm talking about how my life is about to be ruined." Mia sunk farther down into her seat as their teacher, Mr. Haves, continued to talk in an animated voice about something bug-related. Normally Mia liked biology, but then again, she normally had Rob Ziggerman in all his blond, beautiful glory sitting next to her, so what was there not to like? "It's important."

"And leprosy isn't?"

Mia gritted her teeth, once again wishing Candice wasn't such a hypochondriac. This week it was leprosy, the week before it was some weird tapeworm that you could only get from a certain part of the Amazonian rain forest. Which, considering Candice hadn't even left the state of California, was highly unlikely.

"*What?*" Candice raised an eyebrow. "Why are you looking at me like that? I'm serious. My arm could fall off by tomorrow."

"Yes, it could. *If in fact you had leprosy.* All you've got is a bad case of dry skin." Mia forced herself to keep her voice low. "Now, can we please start focusing on my crisis? Did you find out anything?"

"Fine." Candice let out an exaggerated sigh and reluctantly pulled her sleeve down. "So this is what I heard. When Samantha broke up with Trent three weeks ago, she assumed that the guys would be lining up to ask her out. Unfortunately, she forgot to take into account that while she might have a hot body from doing all that cheerleading, she still has a major personality flaw—aka, she's a total witch. Anyway, with the senior prom only four days away and still no invitation, she's decided to focus on Rob."

"She doesn't have a prom date and so now she wants

mine?" Mia wailed as she felt her stomach churn in a way it hadn't done since she had first heard that *Buffy* was going to be canceled.

"Looks like it," Candice agreed in a whisper as Mr. Haves turned off the lights and started to fiddle with his laptop until a picture of a cockroach flashed up on the whiteboard.

"But that's so unfair. Why would he take me out on six perfect dates"—*well, okay, five actually, because going to watch him practice football probably didn't count as a date in the technical sense of the word*—"and then ask me to the prom, if he was going to run off with Samantha Griffin the minute she looked his way and tossed her hair? I mean, he said I was cute and that he liked the fact I wasn't high-maintenance. He said it was refreshing."

"He also said that Indiana was the capital of India in geography the other day," Candice pointed out.

"Okay, so he's not exactly a brainiac," Mia conceded. "But unlike most of the other jocks around here, he doesn't think he's God's gift to the world, either. He's just a regular guy who is sweet and kind—"

"And has abs that would make David Beckham weep," Candice added, and Mia found herself nodding. Yup. There was no denying that Rob Ziggerman was gorgeous. With a capital GORGEOUS. None of which was helping with the problem at hand.

"So where does this leave me?" Mia stared unhappily at the back of Rob's head. His blond hair was styled in a sculptured mess that she longed to run her fingers through (not that she would, of course, because despite being sweet and kind, he did have a thing about his hair). Sitting as close as she could get, Samantha was leaning all over him, leaving no doubt about what her intentions were.

"With a spare prom dress?" Candice guessed before shooting her an apologetic grimace. "Look, you've lived across the street from Samantha for the last ten years, so you know as well as I do that what Samantha wants, Samantha gets. Just accept it and be happy you dated a football player for a few weeks."

"Well, she's not going to get her own way this time. No way." Mia gave a firm shake of her head. "We just need to think of a plan. Ooh, maybe if I start using makeup and do my nails, I can beat Samantha at her own game."

"That's your plan?" Candice peered at her from under her mascara-free eyelashes as if to remind Mia that their makeup kits didn't consist of much more than Clearasil and lip gloss. Then Mia glanced back to where Samantha was now laughing at something Rob had said, and she felt her resolve strengthen.

"It's not such a dumb idea," Mia defended. "I mean, it's a slight problem that I don't have a PhD in eyeliner application, but how hard can it be? Besides, I could always ask Grace to help."

"You hate your sister," Candice reminded her. "And more to the point, Grace hates you. Plus, she's friends with Samantha.

It's that whole cheerleading-club thing. She would never go along with it."

"True," Mia reluctantly agreed as she realized no good could come from telling her fifteen-year-old, pom-pom-wielding, vacuous-Barbie-doll sister about this. "But I've got to do something or I'll be the laughingstock of the school. I mean, how can I go to the prom if Rob dumps me?"

"Oh yes, how embarrassing to not have a prom date. We wouldn't want that," Candice bristled, and Mia found herself wincing in guilt. They'd made a pact to go to the senior prom together to prove they didn't need guys to have fun. Though in all fairness, they'd made this decision based purely on the fact that with Candice's ongoing medical obsession and Mia's encyclopedic knowledge of anything *Buffy*- and *Angel*-related, neither of them had any expectations of being asked in the first place. Let alone by a guy like Rob Ziggerman.

"Candice, I didn't mean that." Mia shot her friend an apologetic look. "It's just, if he hadn't asked me, then no one would've cared less if I did or didn't have a date. But now. . ."

"But now, instead of everyone just thinking you're that weird girl who once tried to get the school to have a Joss Whedon day, they'll think you're the girl Rob dumped," Candice finished, and Mia let out a groan.

"I've really screwed up, haven't I?"

"No, you haven't," Candice finally relented. "Your only sin was being so refreshingly adorable that Rob couldn't resist you."

"Thanks." Mia shot her friend an appreciative glance and sighed. "Now if only I could figure out how to make it happen all over again."

"Got it," Candice suddenly whispered. "Since Rob seems incapable of taking his eyes off Samantha's disgustingly low-cut top, we have to assume that boobs are his fatal flaw. So what about getting a push-up bra to help distract him? We could cut the next few classes and go to the mall."

"But the senior assembly is this afternoon." Mia looked at her friend in surprise. "That's when the football team will be getting their awards. Rob will be there."

"Yes, and if you don't act soon, you'll get to see Samantha and her thirty-six-Ds bouncing up to congratulate him afterward," Candice said in a matter-of-fact way.

"You're right." Mia glanced down at her own less-than-impressive chest. "A push-up bra it is, and maybe we could also—"

"Maybe you could both pay attention?" someone suggested in a mild voice, and Mia looked up to where Mr. Haves had suddenly appeared by her side. "So, Mia, would you like to tell us what happens next?"

Mia hoped no one had heard her push-up-bra plan as she looked up at his encouraging smile. Normally, when teachers did that it was because they were evil passive-aggressive maniacs who liked to see students squirm, but Mr. Haves just genuinely seemed to like helping kids learn. Which as a rule was a good thing, just not today. She peered over to the whiteboard, where there was an amplified photo of a cockroach. Gross.

"Well?" Mr. Haves continued. "What do you think is going to happen to our friend, *Periplaneta americana* next?"

"Um... it's going to fly away?" she guessed, and then wished she hadn't as the sound of Samantha Griffin's unmistakable snicker sounded out. Which was more than a little annoying since Samantha wasn't exactly an A-plus sort of student.

"Not quite. Can anyone else tell me?" Mr. Haves looked hopefully around the class, but when no one raised a hand, he glanced in the direction of his favorite student, Chase Miller—aka the new boy. Well, he'd been at Newbury High for about six months now, but for some reason Mia had never really talked to him. Apparently he was from Boston or some-where like that. He was tall with short light brown hair and green eyes that were set above a pair of razor-sharp cheek-bones. He also tended to keep to himself.

"The jewel wasp is going to put venom into the cockroach's brain so it can control its mind and body, making it a brainless minion."

Okay, and now she remembered why she never talked to him, because he was weird. After all, who in their right mind would know stuff like that?

"Excellent. Well done, Chase." Mr. Haves clapped as he walked back to the front of the room and brought up the next photograph. "The jewel wasp will lay its eggs on the cockroach. After the eggs hatch, the larvae will feed on the roach. Then the larvae use the roach's abdomen as the perfect living-dead incubator until the newly hatched wasps can feed on—"

Much to Mia's relief, the rest of his words were drowned out as the bell rang, quickly followed by the sound of scraping chairs that echoed around the room.

"Can you wait for me? I won't be long." Mia turned to where Candice was busy studying something on her cell phone.

"Sure." Her friend gave a vague wave of her hand without looking up and so Mia piled her books into her bag and took a moment to pat her shoulder-length brown hair into place before hurrying toward Rob. However, just before she got there, Mr. Haves appeared in front of her.

"Mia, could I have a quick word, please?"

"Oh." She gulped as she watched Rob stride out, engrossed in something Samantha was saying, the faint smell of his cologne catching in her nose as he went. Mia realized this probably wasn't the time or the place. "Uh, I guess so."

"Actually, I'll meet you outside." Candice waved her phone in the air. "I've got to make an important call. When it comes to leprosy, you've got to move quickly."

"Did she just say 'leprosy'?" Mr. Haves lifted a surprised eyebrow as he beckoned Mia to follow him to the front of the classroom.

Thanks, Candice.

"Yeah, Leprosy. They're, uh, this great band. She wants to

get concert tickets," Mia improvised as she reluctantly headed over.

"I'll have to listen out for them," Mr. Haves said as he reached into his desk and pulled out a piece of paper, which bore a striking resemblance to the test she'd taken a couple of weeks ago. That was the day after Rob had asked her to the senior prom. Then he waved a second piece of paper in the air. That one looked like Friday's test. The one she'd taken after hearing the rumors that Samantha was after Rob.

"So, about these," Mr. Haves said as Mia studied her shoes. As she recalled, she didn't exactly nail either of them. "I don't need to tell you you're one of my better students, which is why I'm concerned about these grades. Is there something going on?"

What? Like the fact that the guy she'd secretly had a crush on for four years suddenly asked her out on a date for no apparent reason? And then after five more dates, he had made her the happiest girl in the whole entire world by asking her to prom. *And now he had apparently decided to get with Samantha Griffin.*

"Everything's fine. I've just been a bit stressed. It's no biggie," she said.

"Are you sure?" Mr. Haves wrinkled his eyes together and looked concerned. "Because I noticed Rob is now lab partners with Samantha. Does that have something to do with it?"

What? Why? What had he heard?

"No, of course not," she said instead as the blood started to pound in her ears. If Mr. Haves knew about it, then there was a fair chance that the rest of the school did, as well. "And I'm sorry about the tests. I, er, had food poisoning last week."

"What sort?"

"Excuse me?"

"What sort of food poisoning?"

"The poison sort. Anyway, if that's everything, I'd better get going."

"Of course, but remember Mia, if you ever have any problems, you can talk to me. You're a bright student and that's the way we want things to stay. Actually, if you'd like, I could arrange for another student to tutor you before the next test. Just to get you back on track."

"Honestly, Mr. Haves, it's fine. I've got everything completely under control." Mia managed to shoot him a faint smile before she walked out of the classroom. She was about to become the laughingstock of the entire school, and she was fairly certain talking to a teacher or getting some tutoring wasn't going to change that.

"So how bad?" Candice demanded the minute Mia stepped into the hallway and shut the door behind her.

"Bad," she said with a shudder. "Not only did I fail the last two tests, but even Mr. Haves has noticed that Rob and Samantha are getting close. This is serious, Candice. I think we're going to need more than a push-up bra to fix it."

two

"So what's the new plan?" Candice asked as she fired up the brand-new VW Bug that her parents had bought her for her birthday and carefully reversed out of the school parking lot. All Mia got for hers was the promise she could drive her mom's more modest Ford Focus on the weekends. It wasn't quite the same thing.

"I have no idea, so all suggestions will be gratefully received," she said as Candice headed into the Twilight Zone's afternoon traffic and toward the mall. Actually, the town was officially called Newbury, but since nearly all the streets had been named after solar and lunar occurrences, it had long ago been dubbed the "Twilight Zone" as a joke, since nothing much ever happened there.

"Well, we'll think of something. The important thing is not to panic, because it's totally counterproductive. This one time I thought I had this weird lung disease that you can only get when you're ninety. I can't tell you how much I freaked out."

"Right now I'd rather be ninety than stuck with this problem." Mia leaned forward and put some music on, which Candice immediately turned down. She claimed that loud music didn't go with road safety, and with her limited life expectancy, she couldn't afford to take any chances. "How did this even happen to me?"

"It's because you got sick of living in the shadow of your younger sister and when Rob asked you out, the urge to be popular momentarily killed off all of your other brain cells," Candice bluntly informed her, while slowing the car to a snail's pace as they came up to a red light. "It's definitely a character flaw."

"I know. What was I thinking?" Mia slumped back into the plush upholstery and groaned. Candice was right. She had made a cardinal error. Most of the time she was content to live in Fringeland—doing okay at school, staying off the radar, and watching a little bit too much television. She liked Fringeland. She was happy there. But then when Rob had borrowed some biology notes and randomly decided to ask her out (on an *American Idol* night), she had lost all sense of reason and let herself get caught up in the idea of dating one of the most popular guys in school. *And had she mentioned how gorgeous he was?* Even thinking about him made her face start to flush.

"I think we've just established that you weren't thinking," Candice reminded her.

"God, Grace is never going to let me live this one down.

Not that she really believed Rob had asked me in the first place. She said he only did it as a dare."

"That's because Grace is an idiot. I think it's all the hair dye she uses. I read this article the other day, and apparently the chemicals can leak into your brain and make you go crazy. Would explain a lot."

"Yes, but after six dates with me, Rob wants to move on to Samantha, so maybe she's right?"

"Oh, please. Since when is Grace right? Anyway, this is a matter of principle. He asked you to the prom first and he should stick to his decision," Candice declared as she pulled up to the Newbury Mall. It had been built five years ago and was a huge sprawling creation, flanked by palm trees and settled smack-bang in the middle of the Twilight Zone. It was also the place where Mia had finally found her prom dress last week.

She and Candice had spent the entire day trying on clothes and were just about to go home and recover in front of *Supernatural* repeats when she had spotted the most amazing nip-waisted black dress. Candice called it "Goth prom." Mia called it "perfect," and they both agreed that it was worth every cent of the jaw-dropping price. Perhaps Mia should check if the store did refunds?

"So any other ideas besides a push-up bra?" Mia asked as her friend slowed down at the first parking spot, but after studying it for a minute, she obviously thought it looked too difficult to reverse into and kept driving.

"Some slutty shoes?"

"I think it's going to take more than that." Mia frowned. "The way Samantha was operating on him, nothing short of a lobotomy will stop him from falling under her spell. She's like one of those gross wasps that Mr. Haves was talking about. The ones who inject venom into someone's brain and make them become a mindless slave."

"That's it." Candice suddenly put her foot on the brake as the car behind them started to honk. "A spell. We get a spell and make him fall in love with you. Perfect."

"Brilliant idea!" Mia said with a hint of sarcasm. "And if only we went to Hogwarts, then maybe we could figure out how to rustle one up. Seriously, we need to think of something real that will work—"

"Actually." Her friend coughed as she started to slowly drive toward the parking-lot exit. "I think I know what we need. . . ."

"Okay, if this is some sort of joke, it's not funny," Mia said fifteen minutes later as Candice pulled to a stop outside a questionable strip mall that had seen better days not to mention better tenants.

"Of course it's not a joke." Candice sounded offended as she hopped out of the car.

"So what could we possibly find in a liquor store or a seedy video store to help my situation?" Mia demanded as she glanced around at the run-down buildings in front of her.

"This is where we can get a love spell." Candice nodded for

her to follow her past an overflowing Dumpster and around the corner to an alley that was wedged in between a greasy-looking pizza place and a loan shark with blacked-out windows and a kicked-in door.

She had to be kidding.

Mia stared at her friend for a minute, but Candice just hurried on, carefully stepping over the puddles of water that were blocking the way, until she came to a halt outside an unassuming paint-chipped red door.

"Enough." Mia folded her arms in annoyance. "Candice Bailey, this isn't funny, and if you think for one minute that I'm stepping into that place, you're very much mistaken. I thought you were trying to help me, not freak me out."

"I am trying to help." Candice pushed the door open and gripped Mia's wrist.

"What? By taking me to a store that happens to be down a dank, dark alley," Mia snapped as she found herself being dragged into a low-lit room. Through the thick fog of incense that caught in her nose, she could just make out shelf after shelf of bottles and books. *And was that a cauldron over in the corner?*

"Anyway, you're the one who can practically quote *Buffy* and *Supernatural* by heart," Candice reminded her. "You should feel right at home here."

"No, I feel at home in my bedroom when I'm watching those shows on television. There is a big difference," Mia corrected, and was just about to turn around and head out the door when there was a noise. She glanced over to the counter, where an ancient woman with wild silver hair was waving with arthritic fingers.

"Candice, you're back. I'll just go get your latest order," the old woman said as she awkwardly got to her feet and hobbled away.

"Thanks, Algeria." Candice beamed as she tugged Mia over to the counter.

"Excuse me, but why exactly are you on a first-name basis with a five-hundred-year-old witch?" Mia hissed in a low voice the minute the other woman had disappeared behind a beaded curtain with a picture of Elvis on it. "What's going on?"

"Okay, *fine*." Candice let out an exaggerated sigh. "So sometimes orthodox medicine is incapable of dealing with all of my medical problems and I need to look outside the box for cures."

"And by 'outside the box,' you mean in a weird shop that's run by an old woman who looks like she was shipped over on the *Mayflower*?" Mia said as she glanced around the place and shuddered.

"You see, now that's exactly the reason I didn't mention it to you before, in case you went all judgmental," Candice retorted. "Besides, I'll have you know that Algeria is a gifted herbal- ist—and so what if she's a little bit on the wrinkled side? The important thing is that she understands how to heal people with delicate constitutions such as my own."

"How did you even find a place like this?" But before

Candice could answer, Algeria shuffled back into the room with a brown paper bag. Up close and personal she was even older and more shriveled than Mia had first realized, and her blue eyes were so pale they were almost transparent.

"Here you go, dear," the old woman rattled. "These are the seaweed and squid supplements you ordered. With your discount that's eighty-five dollars."

Mia's eyes nearly bulged at the price, but Candice didn't even blink as she handed over her platinum credit card. "Actually," she said at the same time, "there was one other thing I was hoping you could help me with. I don't suppose you have any love spells, do you?"

"Love spells?" Algeria narrowed her watery eyes before glancing around to check that the shop was empty (which, unsurprisingly it was, since who in their right mind would go in there except for them?). Then she leaned forward and lowered her voice, "Who told you about that?"

"No one," Candice quickly assured her. "It's just, when I was in here the other day looking for something for my asthma, I overheard a woman asking for a spell to help her win the lottery. I just figured lottery, love, it's sort of the same thing. So do you do them?"

Mia glared at her friend. A lottery spell? She had to be joking, but before she could say anything Algeria leaned even closer.

"Love spells aren't something that you play around with." The old woman shook her head, and her wild hair seemed to stick out even more. While Mia wasn't quite as appearance-obsessed as Grace or Samantha, what would be the harm in Algeria getting a bit of product to tame that frizz down? "Why do you want one?"

"Actually, it's for my friend. *Prom-date problems*," Candice added in a knowing whisper.

"Always is this time of year." The old woman nodded sagely before turning to Mia. "So, girlie, is this something you really want?"

Mia paused for a moment and shot Candice a hesitant look. Did she really want it? Then the humiliation of seeing Rob so easily transfer his affections marched into her mind and started to dance around in a multicolored blur.

Oh, yes, she wanted it, all right.

"Look," she finally answered. "I know it's a pathetic, sexist, lame tradition that I won't care about in ten years, but when Rob asked me to the prom, there was a part of me that wanted to be *that* girl. Just for one night. You know, the girl who gets the guy. The one who buys the great dress to wear, worries about whether her shoes match her purse. I was even going to let my mom fuss with my hair and take some photos." As she stopped talking, she couldn't believe she was actually buying into this love-spell thing.

"Okay." Algeria seemed convinced. "So what sort of spell would you like? We could give him boils. Or make his ears grow every time he tries to make the hanky-panky with anyone else.

That's a good one." The old woman chortled in amusement.

"I'll say." Candice gave Mia an excited nudge. "I told you she was amazing."

Mia stared at Algeria in alarm. "No, nothing like that. Look, he asked me to the prom and now this horrible girl is sniffing around trying to get him to change his mind. All I want is to make sure he doesn't listen to her."

"Oh." For a moment the old woman looked a bit disappointed. "Are you sure?"

"Definitely," Mia assured her.

"Fine, one run-of-the-mill love spell coming up," Algeria muttered as she pulled out a small black velvet book with Elvis on the front. Then she flicked it open and, after studying it for a moment, started to pull a variety of bottles out from under the counter and lined them up.

As Mia watched her, she tried to ignore the fact that this had to be the weirdest thing she and Candice had ever done (and considering they'd met in seventh grade when they'd been relegated to playing the front and back end of a horse in the school play, that was really saying something). But then again, if it worked, it would all be worthwhile, and if it didn't, well, there was always the push-up-bra idea to fall back on.

"Isn't this great?" Candice grinned next to her as Algeria suddenly looked up and pointed a bony finger at them.

"I need a rose quartz. You, girlie, go over and get me one. It's on the top shelf. There is a stepladder in the corner."

"What?" Mia glanced up in alarm at the shelf Algeria was pointing to and felt her heart start to pound in panic. *No one had mentioned anything about climbing.*

"Oh, Mia doesn't do heights," Candice interrupted as she casually walked over and stood on the small ladder so she could reach up to the top shelf, while Mia tried to resist the urge to sit down on the ground and put her head between her legs to stop the dizzy feeling from overtaking her. "Here you go. One rose quartz crystal."

"Don't do heights, eh?" Algeria looked up with interest.

"It's no big deal," Mia assured her as she willed her heartbeat to return to normal. Besides, it was sort of true, since, as long as she wasn't up somewhere high, she was totally fine. According to her mom, she had been like that even as a baby, and while she had no idea what had caused it, she had a healthy respect for the fact that when she was too far up in the air, her heart rate went through the roof, her palms went sweaty, and nausea would normally follow not long after.

"Well, if you ever want something for it, you come back and see me," Algeria said as she started to pour everything into a small wooden bowl. Then after several minutes of singing and arm waving (*And ew, did she just spit in it?*), she poured the liquid into a brown vial and passed it over to Mia before packing several crystals, a silver amulet, and a bag of sand into a large brown paper bag.

"One love spell. Now remember, the trick is to get as close to him as possible when you're doing this."

"Oh." Mia took the vial and gave it a dubious look. "I thought I'd just be able to throw some powder into the air and make a wish."

Algeria put down the pencil she had been using to write out instructions and fixed Mia with a serious glare. "Look, girlie, if you don't want to do this properly, then it's no good in me even selling it to you. You need to be close to him. Do you hear?"

"Of course she does," Candice butted in. "So what if we do it outside his house? Is that close enough?"

"No good, too many walls in between. Closer."

"But I don't know how to get—" Mia started.

"What about the senior class awards assembly?" Candice suddenly blurted. "It's during last period and if we hurry, we can get back there in time to do it while Rob goes up to get his football award. Oh, but will it be a problem that everyone else will be there?"

For a moment Algeria paused as she rubbed her chin. Then she shot them a toothless grin. "No, I don't think that will be a problem at all. Oh, and by the way, the spell costs one hundred dollars."

"One hundred dollars?" Mia yelped in outrage and was almost tempted to turn and leave. The only thing stopping her from doing so was the image of Rob humiliating her and the fact that Candice had suddenly grabbed her by the elbow with a cast-iron grip.

"We'll take it," her friend assured the ancient woman before nudging Mia to get her wallet out.

"Fine." Mia reluctantly handed over her entire savings and tried not to mind that she would no longer be buying patent-red stilettos to go with her dress. The things she did for love.

"So, do I have the best ideas or what?" Candice announced half an hour later as they both peered out from behind the bleachers. Principal Keegan was droning on about how important it was to get the prom queen and king nominations in by tomorrow afternoon because the ballot papers would be passed out on Wednesday.

"Let me get back to you on that once I know if it works or not," Mia retorted as she tapped her fingers and waited for the speech to finish so that Rob could go up and collect his award and she could start her chanting. They'd managed to sneak undetected into the gym just before the assembly had started, which was lucky, because setting the whole thing up had taken longer than she had imagined.

They'd had to find a wooden bowl, pour in the liquid (which did not smell at all nice), sprinkle sand into a circle, and lay out crystals and amulets in some sort of pentagram pattern. Not to mention the three pages of Algeria's messy handwriting to read once Rob was close enough to them. These sorts of things definitely looked easier on television.

"I told you, Algeria is a genius, so of course it will work," Candice insisted. "By the way, have you seen what Mrs. Taylor is wearing today? What is it with that dress?"

"Oh, I know." Mia was instantly distracted as she craned

her head a bit farther up to get another look at their eccentric IT teacher. As she did so, Chase Miller, who was standing right at the back of the assembly, suddenly glanced over in their direction. Crap. Mia grabbed Candice's arm and tugged her back below the bleachers.

"What was that for?" her friend complained. "You know I bruise easily."

"Sorry." Mia cautiously peered up again and was relieved to see that he was no longer looking their way. "I just thought someone saw us. I had no idea doing a love spell would be so stressful."

"Well, it'll be over soon. Anyway, I don't know what you're so worried about. What could possibly go wrong?" Candice said.

Mia paused, but before she could respond, her friend pointed in the direction of the stage.

"Look, the football team is lining up to get their awards. It's time to get chanting."

three

"*L*ike seriously, you are so dead," Grace said later that afternoon. Mia, who had been in the middle of looking out her bedroom window at Samantha's house, turned around to where her younger sister was standing in the doorway with her hands on her hips in a ridiculous and highly exaggerated pose. "I heard you cut school this afternoon, and Mom's going to flip when she finds out."

"Of course I didn't cut school, and can you get out of my room?" Mia crossed her fingers, since no good could come from Grace knowing what she and Candice had been up to. She returned her attention to the window. It was now almost five in the afternoon and there was no sign of Rob's SUV outside Samantha's house, which had to be a sure sign the spell she'd done earlier had really worked. *Right?*

"Oh, really, well that's not what I heard. And do I smell smoke?" Grace persisted as she walked into the room, her perfect nose wrinkled as if trying to search out a phantom cigarette. All Mia could guess was that the sickly incense from Algeria's store was still clinging to her clothes. She'd better change before dinner, or else her mom would really flip and give them the "Your grandfather died of lung cancer at the age of sixty-one" lecture. Again.

"I'm surprised you can smell anything with all that perfume you're wearing," she shot back, but Grace was undeterred as she continued to prowl around Mia's room looking distastefully at the large David Boreanaz poster on the wall. "Besides, don't you have a huge math test tomorrow that you should be studying for?"

"Oh, that." Grace shrugged her slim shoulders. "I have a feeling I'm going to be sick tomorrow."

"There's nothing wrong with you."

"Of course there is," Grace assured her before doing an Oscar-winning cough, and Mia rolled her eyes. Her sister had probably spent longer perfecting the cough than it would've taken to just study for the test. And even worse was the fact their mom would not just let her off school but probably get a couple of tubs of low-cal Ben and Jerry's just to make sure she was comfortable. Mia blamed the divorce. She had been eight at the time, but Grace had only been six and had cried for weeks for their dad to come home. Their mom was obviously still trying to compensate. None of which improved Mia's mood.

"Just go away, Grace."

"Fine." Her sister shrugged. "I just need to get your laptop first."

"Not likely," Mia retorted as she reluctantly dragged her gaze away from the window. "Use your own computer."

"Mine doesn't have video software on it."

"Since when do you need video software?" Mia widened her eyes in surprise.

"Don't worry, geek-head. I don't have any plans to make up *Buffy* and *Angel* collages and post them on YouTube with stupid emo songs playing in the background." Grace gave a dismissive wave of her hand as she strutted over to where Mia's laptop was sitting. "I just need to do some homework."

"I don't think so." Mia glared. *And there was nothing wrong with her collages. One of them had over ten thousand hits already.*

"Oh, come on. It's not like you're going to need it tonight, anyway, since you'll be too busy moping."

"What's that supposed to mean?" Mia blinked, since even for her sister that was pretty random.

"You know. Samantha and Rob hooked up. She was talking about it at cheerleading practice," Grace informed her, and Mia felt her stomach plummet to the floor. So much for her spell. It had all been for nothing. "I guess it takes five dates with you to let a guy really see what he wants in a girlfriend. Like it's any surprise?" Grace gave a dismissive glance at Mia's outfit.

"Six dates if you count football practice, and besides, there's nothing wrong with what I'm wearing." Mia's disappointment turned to annoyance. "Just because I like to cover my legs and not flash my butt does not make me a loser."

"Yeah, right." Grace rolled her baby blues as if Mia was wearing some sort of mismatched outfit instead of her boy-friend-cut jeans, a cute apple-green T-shirt, and her favorite patterned Converse. "Anyway, I can't begin to imagine how humiliating it must feel to have Rob Ziggerman publicly dump you."

"He hasn't dumped me." *Yet.* "And why does it bother you so much? Worried that some guys might actually want to date girls who have more brains than bounce?"

"Do I look worried?" Grace said as she pushed her chest forward again. Mia sighed. Sometimes it was impossible to believe they were related. Actually, scrap the "sometimes."

"No, but only because you know that if you frown, your face might start to wrinkle," Mia retorted in what was probably the lamest comeback ever, and unsurprisingly, Grace ignored it.

"Whatever. Besides, if Rob really is still taking you to the prom, then why did I just see him go into Samantha's house?" Grace shot her a sickly smile and Mia felt her stomach drop again as she turned back to the window just to confirm that Rob's SUV was indeed parked in the driveway, the late-afternoon sun reflecting off the fender.

How could he?

More importantly, why on earth had she thought that using a stupid love spell would actually work? She must've been suffering some sort of temporary insanity.

"I'm sorry." Grace smirked. "I didn't quite catch your answer to why he's over there."

"He's probably just helping her with homework. Mr. Haves gave us loads of biology stuff to do," Mia said with more confidence than she felt.

"Oh, right. *Homework*." Grace sneered in a totally annoying way, and Mia felt the last of her hope flee the room, since homework wasn't exactly Rob's specialty.

"But I don't even understand why she's interested in Rob in the first place." Mia groaned. "They've all been in the same clique for years, so why hasn't she tried to date him sooner?"

"God, you are so clueless." Grace folded her arms. "If you didn't spend so much time watching TV and hanging out with your weirdo friends, then you might actually realize what's going on."

"What's that supposed to mean?" Mia looked at her sister blankly.

"Okay, fine. So last month Rob was only a prom-king outsider. I mean, he's a football player and he's cute and all, but these days that's not enough. However, with Trent getting busted for drugs, Owen Little coming down with mono, and Jed Mayer losing his scholarship for next year and getting suspended, suddenly Rob has gone from outsider to sure thing."

"But that's insane," Mia spluttered. "Samantha Griffin wants to ruin my life just so that she can date a guy who she *thinks* might be prom king?"

"The only insane thing was that he asked you out in the

first place. It goes against the laws of nature. Rob is popular and hot and you're, well . . . not." Grace shrugged as she sauntered over, grabbed the laptop, and left the room. Then, as the reality of what her sister said started to sink in, Mia pulled her curtains and flicked on her television. When the going got tough, the tough watched *Buffy* Season Two DVDs.

"He *what?*" Candice squealed the next morning as they both stood at Mia's locker. "But that doesn't make sense. What about the spell?"

"I think we can safely assume it didn't work," Mia said in a low voice as she grabbed her books. She didn't even bother to touch her *Supernatural* poster for luck, since not even the gorgeous Winchester brothers could help her now. "Rob's SUV was parked outside Samantha's house for over three hours."

"Man. That sucks." Candice shook her red hair in annoyance as they both headed toward their biology class. "You know, if Algeria wasn't so great at making vitamin infusions, I would totally boycott her on your behalf."

"I guess I was dumb for thinking it would work in the first place. Maybe I really do watch too much TV? I mean, a normal person wouldn't really believe something like that could work."

"I was on this medical Web site the other day, and apparently there is no such thing as a normal person, so quit being so hard on yourself," Candice commanded as they both sat down at a lab bench and Candice systematically lined up the numerous dark brown vitamin bottles she always carried with her. "Now, let's see. Cod liver for my bones. Bach flower remedy for my stress levels, and finally my placebo tablets."

"You do realize what placebo means, don't you?" Mia pointed out.

"Of course, but I just like to cover all my bases." Candice shrugged. Mia shook her head in amazement while she watched Candice finish taking her pills and put the bottles away just before Mr. Haves walked in and smiled at them all.

"Right, class. So if you enjoyed yesterday's lesson about the cockroach and the jewel wasp, you're going to like this one. It's all about parasites that do the same thing to their host. In particular, there is a hairworm that lives in a grasshopper, and when it wants to get out and into water, it gets the grasshopper to jump into ponds and pools, despite the fact that in doing so, the grasshopper will drown."

Ew. Mia shuddered.

"But before we start, let's do a roll call." Mr. Haves opened up a book and started to call out names, but when he got to Chase Miller's name, there was no answer. He stopped and looked around. "Chase Miller?" he repeated. "Has anyone seen Chase?"

"Seen him? I've never even heard of him," Samantha called out, and a few people started to laugh.

"He's that new guy," someone else informed her.

"Oh, right. I thought his name was Chance." Samantha wrinkled her nose for a minute and then shrugged.

"That's probably not the best way to get him to vote you in as prom queen," Candice retorted, but before Samantha could reply, Mr. Haves clapped his hands.

"That's enough. So no Chase." He made a mark and continued calling out names before again frowning as he got to the end of the list. "And finally, Rob Ziggerman?"

"He's not here—" Samantha started to say in a territorial sort of way, but before she could finish, Rob appeared in the doorway looking all kinds of gorgeous in an Abercrombie & Fitch sweatshirt that really brought out the blue in his eyes.

"Hey, Mr. H, sorry I'm late. Coach wanted to talk to me."

"Fine, Rob. Why don't you take a seat and we can get started."

"Sure." Rob gave him a cheery smile and then started to head over toward . . . *her and Candice?*

"Oh my God," Mia said out of the side of her mouth. "Am I seeing things, or is he actually coming over here?"

"Well, judging by the invisible daggers Samantha seems to be throwing at you, I'm going to say yes." Candice started to grin, and Mia felt her mouth drop open in surprise.

"Hey, Mia." Rob came to a halt and nodded at the empty chair next to her. "So is anyone sitting there?"

"Er, n-no," Mia managed to stammer as she felt her heart rate increase. It had worked. It had really worked. Results! And props to Algeria. It seemed the old woman really did know her stuff. She would never judge a person by their warts and facial hair again.

"Cool." He gave her an easy smile and sat down next to her, while Mr. Haves fiddled with his laptop at the front of the class. "By the way, I'm sorry I didn't sit next to you yesterday. Samantha said she was having some major freak-out over her biology notes and wanted me to help her. I even had to go around there yesterday afternoon, but she still couldn't get it. I told her we should just go across the street and see you because you're a total whiz at bio, but she didn't seem to like the idea."

"I bet," Candice muttered under her breath from Mia's other side.

"So you really were helping her with homework?" She ignored her friend as she stared at Rob's sincere face.

"Yeah, though between you and me, I don't think she was really trying very hard. Anyway, before I forget, I got you these." He slipped a packet of Ho Hos over to her as Mr. Haves continued to talk about suicidal grasshoppers. "I just saw them and thought of you. Oh, and by the way, you still haven't told me what color your dress is. I want to make sure I get the corsage just right."

Mia stared at the small cakes before peering back up at Rob. Then she started to grin. Was this just turning into the best day ever?

By the end of the day, Mia still felt like she was floating about ten feet off the ground as she continued to clutch at the Ho Hos. They might've only been on six dates, but she knew enough about Rob Ziggerman to realize the importance of the cream-filled chocolate cakes, because apart from his hair and his football, Rob loved his food. Especially anything that had Hostess on the package.

She arrived at her locker and was just about to dial her combination when the door swung open. Well, that was weird. She put her head in and stared at the neatly stacked books that were piled up in alphabetical order. Okay, that was even weirder. She didn't bother to keep her beloved DVDs in order; she was hardly going to start doing it to her locker. Besides, as she often told her mom, it wasn't a mess, it was just organized chaos. There was a difference. Anyway, it had obviously gotten to Candice, and for some strange reason she must've decided to clean up.

She shut the door and walked out to the parking lot where she was meeting Candice, but when there was no sign of her distinctive VW, Mia pulled out her cell phone and called her.

"Hey, you forgot to shut the door on my locker today," she said the minute Candice answered.

"I wasn't in your locker."

"You weren't?" Mia said in surprise.

"No, remember you changed your combination after I left my homeopathic flu powder in there. You were worried Principal Keegan would think you were dealing drugs."

"Oh, yeah." Mia frowned. "Well it just seems like someone has been in there."

"Did they take anything?"

"I don't think so. Though for some strange reason they cleaned it up." Not that she was really too concerned since it was so easy to break into the lockers that she never kept anything important in there.

"That's not strange, that's madness," Candice retorted. "I've seen inside your locker and it's not pretty."

"Yeah, well it is now. Anyway, where are you? I thought we were meeting here."

"Sorry, I decided to skip sixth period and go to the mall."

"Oh, is this part of the great earring debate? I still like the silver ones best. Especially if you're going to have your hair up. Actually, you should've told me—I would've skipped with you. IT was totally boring, and besides, I'm still too excited about the fact the spell worked. Can you believe . . . *ugh, what is that chewing noise?*"

"Oh, that's me," Candice apologized. "I'm just finishing off my beef jerky."

"Beef jerky?" Mia blinked as she tried to ignore the loud masticating sound coming from the other end of the phone.

"That's right," Candice agreed. "It's medicinal. I've been thinking my iron levels are getting a bit low, and you know I have to be careful not to become anemic."

"Yes, but you don't eat red meat," Mia reminded her before frowning. "Anyway, can't you just take pills for that?"

"Jeez Mia, what's with the twenty questions?"

"Sorry," she said in surprise, since normally there was nothing Candice liked more than to talk about her ongoing preventative health regime. "Anyway, should I meet you at the mall? I still need shoes."

"No, I'm just about to leave for my acupuncture appointment, but we could go check them out tomorrow. Okay? I gotta go. Bye," Candice said before ending the call.

Mia closed her phone and was just contemplating whether to call her mom and see if she could wrangle a lift—or else face the school bus—when someone coughed behind her. She spun around to see Chase Miller looking at her intently.

"Uh, hi?" she said in surprise as she tried to figure out if there was a particular reason he was standing there. Then she recalled that he hadn't been in class that morning. Perhaps he wanted her notes? Which could be a problem since all she had written down was a series of love hearts with the initials RZ in the middle of them. "Can I help you with something?"

"Yeah, Mia—look, I know we haven't really talked before, but this is kind of important," he said as he awkwardly rocked from one foot to another and appeared to be chewing his lip. Then she let out an inward groan as she remembered Mr. Haves's suggestion to help her get back on track for the next biology test. Chase had obviously been roped in to do the honors.

"Is this about the tutoring? Because I told Mr. Haves that those last two tests were just accidents and I'm fine. Anyway, thanks. It was nice of you to offer."

He shook his head, confused. "That's not why I'm here."

"Oh, it's not?" She studied his face to try and get a clue about what he wanted, but his pale green eyes weren't giving much away.

"Actually, it's about the spell you did yesterday."

"What?" Mia yelped as she glanced around her to check that none of the other students who were flooding out of the school had heard what he just said. "O-of course I didn't do a spell. That's just crazy talk." She looked at his face to see if he bought her bluff. "W-why would you even say something like that?"

"Because I know a spell was done at Newbury High at the exact time I saw you behind the bleachers at the senior awards assembly yesterday," he said, and Mia let out a groan. *So that would be a "no" for buying her bluff, then.*

"I told you, I don't know what you're talking about." She tried to sound convincing, but Chase just gave her a stubborn glare.

"Look, all I need is the incantation you used." He folded his arms and Mia shot him an annoyed frown.

"Why? So you can tell the whole school I did a love spell? Besides, it wasn't *really* a love spell, because that would imply Rob didn't like me and he did—er, does. I mean, we had six dates together. It's just ever since Samantha decided to steal him from me he's been a bit . . . distracted. So really the spell was just to help jog his memory. A reminder spell, you could say. And it totally worked." She held up the Ho Hos as proof, and Chase stared blankly at her for a moment before rubbing his chin.

"Okay, the thing is, it doesn't really matter what sort of spell you think you did, because—"

"It might not matter to you, but it matters to me." Mia bristled as she thought about her adorable dress that was hanging in her closet in preparation for Friday night. "The whole time I've gone to this high school, people have only ever thought of me as the weird quirky girl who can quote too much *Buffy*. This is my chance to be someone else. Just for one night, so for you to say—"

"Sorry, I didn't mean it like that," he apologized as he ran a hand through his short hair. "I just meant that we have a bigger problem on our hands than whether you thought you did a love spell or a reminder spell."

"Excuse me?" She looked at him blankly, feeling like she was watching a foreign movie without the subtitles because not a lot of his conversation was making sense.

"What you actually did was an ancient ritual called *Viral Zombaticus*. Unfortunately, there are at least ten different strains of it, which is why I need the specific incantation you used so that I can reverse it."

"You're still not making any sense."

"I'm not doing a very good job of this," he admitted as he took a deep breath. "But what I'm trying to say is that when you did that spell yesterday, you inadvertently turned everyone who was at the assembly into flesh-eating zombies."

four

"I'm sorry, but for a moment there I thought you said 'zombies.'" Mia scratched her chin and stared at him. She was definitely going to have to cut back on her television viewing, because next she'd be seeing vampires around every corner and thinking that Principal Keegan was a demon (which, actually, wouldn't be that much of a stretch, considering his beady eyes and fat nose).

"I did say 'zombies,'" Chase clarified without a hint of a smile. *Oh, right.* Well, at least there was nothing wrong with her hearing, though her brain seemed to be moving a bit slower than normal. She wrinkled her nose and peered around the front of the school to see if there was anyone with a camera, but it was remarkably camera-free. Which meant she still didn't have a clue what was going on.

"Okay, I don't get it," she was finally forced to confess. "Is this some sort of yearbook prank or something? To try and get a photograph of me running away from pretend zombies?

Because, to be honest, you don't strike me as the yearbook type."

"Mia, this isn't a joke," he assured her as he thrust a business card into her hands. "I'm from the Department of Paranormal Containment, and it's my job to get this zombie virus reversed before it moves into stage two, but to do that I really, *really* need the incantation you used. So can you please help me out here?"

Mia took the card and studied it for a minute before she handed it back and started to frown.

"You can't seriously be telling me you work somewhere called the Department of Paranormal Containment. I mean, you're a high-school senior. And even if there were such a place, do you really expect me to believe they give out business cards with gold font on them? So what's this really about?"

"Look, I know this is a lot to take in, and if I had more time I'd love to explain it to you, but right now I really am in a rush."

"So give me the CliffsNotes version." Mia folded her arms and shot him a stubborn glare.

"Fine," he relented. "The Department of Paranormal Containment is a government organization that works covertly to deal with anything out of the ordinary. And by that, I mean paranormal. We have agents all over the world who fight everything from demons to banshees. The department's sole purpose is to keep the balance between good and evil from being disturbed. And unless you let me have that incantation, team evil will definitely be gaining a few points on us."

"Right." Mia couldn't quite hide her incredulity. "So you're trying to tell me that you work for a secret organization and you need to get rid of all the zombies I created?"

"That is correct," he deadpanned.

"Well, no offense, but I think you can probably take the afternoon off since, as you can see, we're a zombie-free school," Mia replied, looking around the school and parking lot that was quickly emptying out. "Oh, and in case you have any buddies who want to hunt vampires and werewolves, then you can tell them not to bother, either."

"You do know that vampires and werewolves aren't real, don't you?" He raised an eyebrow in her direction.

"Oh, but zombies are? So why can't I see any?"

"That's because the virus works in four stages," he explained in a patient voice, though Mia couldn't help but notice his fists were clenched. "Stage one lasts about thirty hours and the infected people are relatively harmless, though on the inside the virus is slowly taking over. Stage two is when the skin starts to lose its elasticity, the victims begin to uncontrollably crave meat, and their bodies start to shut down; occasionally, those who are already ill can die of organ failure at this point. Stage two goes on for up to another thirty hours."

Mia stared at him. He could not be serious. However, he seemed unperturbed by her reaction as he continued.

"When they reach stage three, they fall into a short coma and then move into stage four. It takes about two hours after the coma for the body to fully adjust, but when it does, they will become dead, mindless creatures powered only by rage and their need to feed on living flesh."

"And let me guess." Mia raised an eyebrow at him. "If I give you the incantation, you can cure everybody before it gets to stage two and no one will be any the wiser."

"That is correct."

"More like convenient, since it means you never have to prove if it's real or not."

"It's real," Chase said in a tight voice as he glanced at his watch. "And I'm quickly running out of time, so please Mia, can I just have the incantation, because without it we're all going to be in a lot of trouble. So where is it? Is it in your locker?"

"Oh my God." Mia widened her eyes at the mention of her locker. "That was you, wasn't it? You went looking through my locker for it."

"Of course I didn't." Chase looked offended.

"Well it seems like a big coincidence. Don't tell me Samantha put you up to this. I mean, she looked pretty annoyed before when Rob sat next to me in biology again. Did she ask you to try and find something to blackmail me into breaking up with Rob? Because you know I wouldn't put it past her. And the zombie business is a nice touch, because everyone knows how much I loved *Buffy* and *Angel*."

"What?" He sounded a bit astounded. "Mia, I'm not trying to blackmail you about anything. I thought I just explained why I need it."

"Yes, but it doesn't make any sense." She folded her arms and tried not to panic, but it would be the final nail in her humiliation coffin if anyone found out what she'd done.

"Look, I'm not trying to be difficult here, I just need the incantation." Chase paused for a minute and rubbed his chin. "Okay, so how about this. If you give it to me, then I promise not to say a word to anyone. Is it a deal?"

No, Mia wanted to say, *definitely not*. Especially since she was sure it couldn't be a good thing to encourage his delusions. But then again, since he already seemed to know about the spell, her best option was to humor him and hope he really was true to his word.

"Fine. So if I give you the incantation, then will you promise never to mention it again? Especially not to Samantha," she double-checked, and he gave a vigorous nod of his head.

"I promise." The worry lines around his green eyes seemed to lessen. However, the rest of his words were lost as Mia's phone beeped.

She glanced at the screen and felt her heartbeat start to quicken. It was a text from Rob. *Do u want a lift?* She quickly glanced over to the parking lot and caught sight of Rob's SUV in the far corner. Mia grinned as she quickly reached into her bag, which was only slightly less messy than her locker, and hunted around for the handwritten pages Algeria had given her.

"Here you are." She thrust them into his hands.

"Thank you, Mia. I really appreciate this. Oh, and by the

way, it's important you keep this conversation to yourself. Do you understand that?"

"You have absolutely no worries there," she assured him as she tried to stop her heart from pounding in anticipation. Rob really did still like her.

"Oh, and once this is over, if you do need help with that biology test, I don't mind giving you a hand. It's my best subject." Chase coughed and didn't quite look at her.

"What?" Mia stared at him blankly for a minute before realizing what he was talking about. *And why was he looking so uncomfortable?* "Oh, right. Actually, I should be okay, but thanks for the offer," she called out over her shoulder as she hurried across the parking lot to where Rob was waiting for her.

Zombies? She didn't think so.

"Hey, I didn't realize you knew that guy. Isn't he in our biology class?" Rob asked as Mia climbed up into the front seat.

"Oh, yeah. He just wanted some notes," Mia said, since she had no desire to let him know about the love spell she'd done. Not to mention the fact that while Chase Miller was obviously crazy, if she repeated anything he said, then she might look crazy as well. Right now that wasn't the look she was going for.

"That's one of the things I like about you, Mia—you're always helping other people." Rob started up the SUV and drove east on Sunset Drive as his nose started to twitch.

"Hmmm, have you been eating chicken? It smells good."

"Chicken?" Mia said in surprise as she sniffed her sleeve, but all she could smell was the fabric softener her mom always used. "No, it's not me."

"We must've just passed a restaurant." Rob shrugged before grinning. "Oh, and by the way, did you like my present?"

"You mean the Ho Hos?"

"No, I left you some Twinkies in your locker. I hope you don't mind. I just saw them and couldn't stop thinking about you. Oh, and I cleaned up in there, too. It was a bit messy."

"You cleaned my locker?" Mia said in surprise since . . . well . . . it was sort of odd that he didn't ask her first. But before she could say anything else, Rob gave her the most adorable grin, and she felt her surprise fade away.

"Yeah, I have this thing about mess. I hope you don't mind."

"Cleanliness is next to godliness," she assured him while making a mental note to sort out her bag when she got home. For a moment she felt a stab of guilt for accusing Chase of doing it, but that feeling didn't stay long. Besides, the guy was definitely a few french fries short of a Happy Meal if he thought her love spell hadn't worked, because Rob had given her two cakes and cleaned her locker. He must *really* like her.

Mia was still beaming ten minutes later after Rob dropped her off with the promise that he would see her tomorrow morning. She waited until his SUV had disappeared up the road before heading toward the front door. As she pushed her key into the lock, her nose twitched at the smell of baking, which was weird since her mom normally didn't finish work until well after five.

She dumped her school bag and wandered into the kitchen to where Grace was standing over a tray of cupcakes, her blonde hair piled high on her head and her stub nose smudged with flour.

"And now I've seen everything." Mia lifted a surprised eyebrow as she reached over to a bowl of pink icing. However, before she could stick her finger in, Grace batted it away with a wooden spoon.

"It's not for you," her sister snapped. "But if you want to make yourself useful, you can go and take the next batch out of the oven."

"Since when do you bake? Or eat anything that has calories in it?" Mia stared at her sister and tried to figure out if she had walked into a parallel universe. "Besides, what happened to your life-threatening cough?"

"I made a miraculous recovery," Grace retorted as she stomped over to the oven and opened the door herself. "And since you're not going to help, can you go away please? I've got a lot of work to do."

"I don't think so." Mia shook her head as she caught sight of at least three dozen iced cupcakes sitting over on the table. "I'm far more interested in what has brought out your inner

Martha Stewart. . . . And why do these all have *SG* in the middle of them?"

"I thought that was obvious." Grace shrugged her shoulders as she carried the next batch over to the bench. "It's to help with Samantha's prom-queen campaign tomorrow."

"What?" Mia stared at her sister. "You're helping Samantha Griffin? The girl who tried to steal my prom date and ruin my life?"

"Mia, honestly, I don't know why you take these things so personally. I told you that you're breaking the laws of nature by dating Rob in the first place. Besides, this sort of experience will be invaluable for me when I'm running my own prom-queen campaign."

"You are unbelievable. And what are you going to do with all these if Samantha doesn't get on the ballot?"

"Oh please, don't be so ridiculous. Of course she'll be on there. Samantha is the person guys want to be with and girls want to be."

"Really, because in my experience all the girls I know want to kill her," Mia retorted.

"Yes, but your friends are hardly the movers and shakers of Newbury High." Grace didn't even bother to look up. "Anyway, if you want someone to blame, then go see Principal Keegan since he was the person who barbarically decided to get rid of the prom court and only let nominees have one day to try and canvass for votes."

Mia couldn't even be bothered to respond as she shook her head and left the kitchen. As always, it was completely useless to talk to Grace. Besides, she had her Ho Hos and Rob Ziggerman to think about. Not to mention taking another peek at her dress. Life didn't really get much better than this.

five

"There you are. I've been looking for you everywhere." Candice panted as she came to a halt at Mia's locker the next morning.

"Sorry, I had to catch the bus, because would you believe the entire car was full of the cupcakes that Grace made to help Samantha with her prom-queen campaign and Mom didn't have time to make two trips?"

"Grace is helping Samantha?" Candice arched an eyebrow before frowning. "Why am I not surprised?"

"Yeah, and don't even get me started on the fact that she used my laptop to make up a prom-queen video clip for Samantha's Facebook page. Unbelievable."

"Anyway, this will cheer you up," Candice assured her. "I've got some Oreos for you."

"Why are you giving me cookies?" Mia looked at the double packet her friend was holding out to her.

"Because you like them, of course." Candice shrugged. "Why else?"

"Er, well, I guess that's as good a reason as any," she said as she took the packet and opened up her locker. "And . . . Hey! What's going on?"

"Boy, someone really did tidy up in there," Candice commented as she leaned over Mia's shoulder to see what the problem was.

"Actually." Mia coughed as she stared at the neatly stacked towers of cookies and candy that were now inside it. "I'm talking about why my locker suddenly looks like a bake sale. How are people breaking into it? I've really got to get a new combination."

"Oh, right." Candice wrinkled her nose. "That is weird. Who would do that?"

"I have no idea. Did I miss a memo or a school announcement?" she demanded.

"Of course not." Candice shook her red hair just as Samantha came storming toward her with a scowl etched across her face and her shirt cut even lower than the one she'd been wearing yesterday.

"Mia Everett, I want to talk with you." Samantha came to a halt and put her hands on her hips in an exaggerated pose, while ignoring Candice altogether. "I don't know what you think you're playing at, but it won't work."

"I'm not playing at anything," Mia said brusquely. "Rob asked me to the prom first. Why is that so hard to accept?"

"I'm not talking about Rob." Samantha rolled her mascara-coated eyes in disdain, and Mia blinked.

"You're not?"

"I just came from the office where these were printed so they could be handed out this morning. I want you to explain yourself," Samantha demanded as she pulled a piece of paper out of her bag and thrust it in Mia's face.

"It's a ballot." Mia shrugged. "And I'm guessing it's for the senior prom king and queen. But you know, Samantha, if you're canvassing for votes, here's a tip; it might be a good idea to try the nice approach. I mean, giving out free cupcakes can only get you so far."

"So is that what you've been telling people?"

"What do you mean? Why would I be telling people anything?" Mia stared at her blankly before finally grabbing the ballot that Samantha was still waving around. For a moment she studied it before finally looking up in astonishment. *"I've been nominated for prom queen?"*

"Oh my God," Candice yelped from next to her. "Did you just say 'prom queen'?"

"That's what it says." Mia held up the ballot. "Though how it happened, I have no idea."

"Oh, don't play dumb, Mia. You were obviously gunning for this all along, but if you think for one minute you can come in here and steal my crown, then you've got another think coming. And you can start taking down all those stupid posters, too."

"Posters?" Mia blinked as she glanced around and realized that practically every senior locker was plastered with flyers saying *Vote Mia for Queen*.

"I don't know what you did to suddenly make yourself the focus of everyone's attention, but I can tell you that it's not going to work." Samantha flicked back a lock of golden hair and then glanced at Mia like she was something on the bottom of her shoe.

"Well, if that's the case, then I don't why you are even bothering to talk to me," Mia replied.

"I couldn't agree more, and normally I wouldn't bother to waste my time." Samantha gave a dismissive shrug as she unzipped her Coach purse and pulled out a box of chocolate truffles. "However, I needed to give you these, so I thought I'd kill two birds with one stone. Actually, speaking of birds, can you smell that?"

"Smell what?" Candice's nose twitched.

"Chicken." Samantha leaned forward and sniffed Mia's arm. "Something smells like chicken. I might go to the cafeteria and see if they have any." Then, without saying another word, Samantha turned on her ridiculously high heels and strutted off in the other direction as Mia and Candice turned to each other.

"Wow," they both said at the same time before Candice widened her eyes.

"Hey, I wonder if this has something to do with the spell you did yesterday? Perhaps it didn't just make Rob love you, it made everyone love you? You know, next time we go back there, I think I'd better get one for myself, because if it can make you prom queen, imagine what it could do for my health issues?" Candice's voice was thoughtful as she ripped open another packet of beef jerky.

"Mia, can I talk to you for a moment? We have a problem," a vaguely familiar voice said, and she spun around to where Chase Miller was standing. He was wearing the same jeans he'd had on yesterday, though the retro T-shirt and the bags under his green eyes both seemed fresh.

"Hey, it's New Boy. I didn't know you were friends with him. Actually, I didn't know he was friends with anyone. He doesn't strike me as a talker," Candice pronounced as she waved her beef jerky at him. Then she turned back to Mia and said, "Mind you, I guess talking is overrated, and he sure is tasty looking. I wonder if he has some cookies for you, too?"

"Uh, Mia, this really is important." Chase gave an urgent cough, and Mia wished Candice wasn't talking in such a loud voice.

"I'm thinking Fig Newtons," Candice continued, oblivi- ous to Chase's embarrassment. "Don't ask me why, but he just looks like that sort of guy. Oh, and Mia, don't forget to remind him to vote for you."

"You realize he's right here and can hear you?" Mia said to Candice.

But before she could reply, Chase said, "It's about yesterday. You know the incantation for the spell you gave me—"

"Hey, he knows about the spell?" Candice interrupted in surprise. "Are you sure that's wise? I mean, yes, he's cute, but you know what they say about the quiet ones—"

What? Chase Miller wasn't cute. He was too tall, his hair was too short, and not to mention the fact that he was crazy. Of course he hid it well under his unassuming exterior, but now that Mia knew the truth about him, he wasn't fooling anyone.

"The point is," Chase cut in, "we have a problem. I used the two pages of incantation you gave me along with a reversal potion, and the virus should've been stopped, but for some reason it didn't work."

"Two pages of incantation? I thought there were three?" Candice frowned for a moment. "Because remember it took us a while to decipher her writing. She should think about doing those things on a computer in future. There would be a lot less margin for error."

"You're right." Mia nodded before turning to Chase. "Are you sure I only gave you two?" she asked.

"I'm positive," Chase assured her in a tight voice.

"Oh." Mia frowned. "Well, I wonder where the other one is, then?"

"Probably in your bag," Candice suggested. "It's always such a mess in there you can never find anything. Remember I looked it up on the Internet once because I was worried that you might've had some kind of strange 'messy' disease?" Then she turned to Chase and gave him a reassuring smile. "But it's okay—apparently she's just really untidy."

Mia shot Chase a rueful glance as she pulled open her bag and dug around until she found the extra piece of paper. "Actually, Candice is right—I was getting confused. It's been a bit of a stressful week with this whole Samantha-trying-to-steal-my-prom-date thing. I guess I just made a mistake."

"Look, could I speak to you privately for a minute?" He glanced over to where Candice was engrossed in her beef jerky.

"But didn't you say yesterday that you would leave me alone now?" she reminded him. "Besides, class starts in ten minutes and I really want to try and catch Rob."

"Yes, well yesterday I thought this thing was containable, but since you forgot to give me the complete incantation we have a problem."

Mia rolled her eyes and dropped her voice so it was little above a whisper. "Please tell me you're not still thinking about this zombie business. I mean, yes, I think my spell did do something because everyone is being really nice to me. I can even see why Grace likes being popular so much, because it's cool when people give you things. But honestly, you've got to stop with this crazy idea. These are just regular kids with a healthy disposable income that they want to spend on food for *moi*."

"Just give me five minutes so I can show you something."

"Do we really have to do this again?"

"*Please*, Mia, I just need five minutes," he said desperately in a low voice, cautiously glancing around him.

"Okay, fine." She let out a sigh before turning back to Candice. "Look, I've got to talk to Chase about, er, biology—but I'll see you in class. Save me a seat?"

"Not so fast." Candice narrowed her eyes. "I want to know what's going on between you and . . . Oh, is that a steak sub I can smell? You guys go ahead, I'm just going to the cafeteria to see what's for lunch." Candice trotted off in the other direction.

Okay, that was odd. Candice really had to slow down with the vitamin supplements because they were obviously wreaking havoc on her hormones.

"Well?" She folded her arms once Candice had gone.

"Actually, I don't think the hallway is the best place to talk about it. Let's go in here." Chase headed toward an empty classroom, and Mia rolled her eyes and reluctantly followed him. Once they were inside, he locked the door and pulled his laptop out of his backpack.

"Okay, so what's this all about?" she demanded as she watched him bite into his full bottom lip in concentration.

"In a nutshell, the zombie virus you released has moved into the second stage, which means it is no longer reversible, and by lunchtime on Thursday it will become fully active."

"Ugh, okay, that's enough." Mia held up her hands. "Look, I know I humored you yesterday, but that was because I was preoccupied about Rob. The thing is, you can't keep talking about zombies as if they're real. I mean, seriously, how can you expect me to believe that every single student—"

"And teacher," Chase interjected.

"Fine. That every single student and teacher who was at the senior assembly will turn into a zombie come twelve o'clock Thursday. It's ridiculous."

"Look." He took a controlled breath and seemed to clench his jaw. "I know this is a lot to take in and I know you don't want to believe me, but it's true. Would it help if I gave you some proof?"

"What, like eating my brains or something? No thanks," she retorted before frowning. "And anyway, you were at the senior assembly. I saw you standing at the back rolling your eyes while Rob gave his speech for being football player of the year, which by the way, was very rude of you."

Chase didn't look remotely apologetic as he shrugged. "Yes, you're right, I was there."

"So, if I really did turn everyone into zombies, then why aren't you trying to eat me?" she demanded as Chase ran a frustrated hand through his short hair. *Ha! Try and answer that, crazy boy.*

"I explained how the virus works. Right now everyone is only in stage two. They don't start eating flesh until they hit stage four. As for me, I'm immune to the virus in any form."

"Oh, well, isn't that handy," she replied.

"Actually." He tightened his jaw and Mia blinked in

surprise. If she didn't know better, she would almost say that he was mad. "'Convenient' is the last thing I would call it. I've got a mutant gene, which we think came down through my mom's side. It means that while I can still be killed by a zombie, I can't be infected with the virus, no matter how it is transmitted, nor can I carry it. Unfortunately, less than one percent of the population has the gene and scientists haven't worked out a way to transfer it to anyone else yet."

"And me? Am I going to turn into a zombie?"

"No." Chase shook his head. "You were the one who did the incantation, which makes you immune, too."

"Fine, so I turned everyone into zombies except for you and me, which means you can't prove it. Now, if you don't mind, I'm going to class."

"Mia." He gently grabbed her arm just as she headed for the door and pointed to the laptop. "If you want proof, come and take a look at this. It's an outbreak that we contained last month."

Mia stared at the screen and let out a long groan. "Chase, this isn't proof. It's a YouTube clip."

"That's right. Some idiot filmed us while we were trying to fight. We keep shutting these things down, but someone keeps posting them again. Still, at least I can show you what a zombie looks like."

"You don't expect me to believe that this video is—*gross*, what is that girl doing?"

He leaned in closer to the screen and Mia tried to ignore the way his shoulder brushed hers. For a psycho, he sure smelled nice. "That's what happens when the virus reaches stage four and the person becomes a zombie. The heart is effectively killed and the body is controlled by muscle spasms, which is what makes them walk funny."

"I'm not talking about the walk. It looks like blondie there is eating someone's arm." Mia pulled a face. Whoever had made this thing was a total sicko but brilliant with special effects.

"Yes, that's what zombies tend to do. Eat flesh. Though not brains. That's just an urban myth." He waited until the video had finished before playing another one. This one was equally bad, and Mia felt her eyes widen as she watched a group of ten so-called zombies attack some salesclerks at a mall. Those guys could really scream. And they sure must've blown their budget on ketchup.

Then she caught sight of Chase and a few other men suddenly come in and drag the zombies away. Okay, so this was starting to creep her out a little, and Mia shuddered as she saw a link to another clip.

"What's that one?" She pointed, but Chase just covered the keyboard with his hand.

"You don't need to see that one."

"That's right, because you know it's not going to change my mind about this. I mean, yes, I admit that my spell might've done something, but whatever it was, it's all good. I've been nominated for prom queen and you should see all the booty I've got in my locker. They love me. Rob loves me. It's a win/win."

"No." Chase sighed as he looked at her sadly. "I'm afraid that's not the reason they're being so nice to you."

"Oh, really?" She bristled. "I might not be the most popular girl at this school, but it's not like everyone hates me, either— well, apart from Samantha Griffin, of course. But the point is, why would you think it more likely that they are zombies than that they just like me?"

"Because I've seen it happen before." He clenched his fists into two tight balls. "The reason you've become the focus of everyone's attention is because they want to fatten you up."

"Excuse me?" Mia's hand automatically flew to her stomach as she tried to remember the last time she had done some crunches. She had a prom dress to fit into still, and three days of misery eating to combat. "I'm not sure I follow."

"Mia, you unleashed the zombie virus, and that makes you the queen."

"Great, so I'm queen of the zombies. What does that even mean? Will I be able to command them all in their zombie quest to take over the world?"

"Not exactly." He hit *play* on the final YouTube clip, and she watched hundreds of slow-moving freaks rip apart a middle-aged woman—limb by blood-soaked limb. "I'm sorry, Mia, being a queen isn't a good thing. It just makes you first up on the menu."

six

*M*ia let out a jagged breath as the YouTube clip ended. "You're not lying, are you?" she finally said as she tried to keep her panic from rising.

"I'm sorry." Chase shook his head.

"How did this even happen?" She blinked at him. "I mean, one minute I was doing a love spell and the next minute I'm turning myself into an all-you-can-eat zombie buffet? Maybe Grace is right and it's because I tried to go against the forces of nature to date Rob? After all, she's been popular since she was born, but no one's ever tried to eat her before."

"That's the part I don't understand," Chase admitted as he ran a hand across his smooth jaw. "Normally to work a spell like this, you need incredible focus and concentration, which comes from years of training," Chase said in a soft voice, which somehow managed to calm her down a bit. "Which is why I'm not sure how you managed to achieve it."

"Well, Candice and I did do yoga for a few weeks. Mind

you, that was a little boring so we swapped to Tae Bo. Oh, though I am a Taurus, and we're pretty stubborn—maybe that was it?"

Chase didn't look convinced.

"The thing I still don't understand is, if zombies are real, then how come we don't know about them? I mean, those YouTube clips for a start. Why is it never reported in the news?" Mia wrinkled her nose.

"Because the department always covers up. Trust me, it's in no one's interest to know the truth about what is really out there."

"But how do they even do it? I can barely hide it from my mom when I miss my curfew by ten minutes."

"It really depends on the situation. Sometimes it's blamed on fires, natural disasters, or occasionally a pandemic—which, when you think about it, isn't really too far from the truth. As for people who have survived attacks and the families of those who have been killed or infected, the department uses memory-adjustment techniques. It's sort of like what they do in that movie *Men in Black,* but without the electronic gadgets."

"But that's impossible." She stared at him. This day was getting more surreal by the minute.

"You'd actually be surprised at how easy it is. Who really wants to believe that there are zombies or dragons out in the world?"

"There are dragons?" Mia blinked, and Chase raised an eyebrow as if to prove his point.

"See, people believe what they want to believe."

"So why didn't that work on you?" she asked.

"I guess I don't believe the same things as everyone else." He shrugged, but before she could say anything else, there was a pounding noise, and Mia looked up to see about twenty faces pressed up to the glass panel in the door.

"W-what are they all doing?"

"At a guess, I'd say they're looking for you," he said in his matter-of-fact voice as she suddenly realized why he had locked the door.

"Oh my God." Her alarm turned into blind panic as she reached out and instinctively clutched at his arm. It felt oddly reassuring and she edged closer to him. "It's started? In the movies these things always happen at night. Night is a much better time. Now is not so good."

"It's all right. They're not here to eat you—not *yet*, anyway. You're the zombie queen, which means you're like a magnet for them. As the virus progresses, the pull will get stronger. They're here because you're here. Apparently you are giving off some sort of pheromone. I've heard it smells like chicken."

"Chicken? So that explains why Rob and Samantha both were trying to smell me." Mia shut her eyes for a minute and tried to imagine she was somewhere else. Preferably in a place where she hadn't turned everyone into zombies and they weren't now looking at her like she was a drumstick. Unfortunately, when she opened them again, she was still in an empty classroom with twenty seniors drooling at her from the other side of the door. Popularity definitely had its drawbacks.

"Okay," she said in a low voice as she realized she was still holding on to Chase's arm. She quickly let it go. Smelling of chicken obviously made a person react strangely. "So I think it's probably time we did that reversal spell. Just tell me what you need to do and I'm there. One hundred percent. Because the sooner I stop being on the menu, the better."

Chase seemed to be fixated on something on the wall. "Um, well, it's a bit more complicated than that."

Mia jumped up and stood in between him and his wall viewing so that he could concentrate on what she was saying. "What do you mean?"

"Remember I explained to you yesterday about how the virus worked? Well, it's moved into stage two, and unfortunately, it's now impossible to reverse."

"What?" Mia yelped as she looked at the faces that were still pressed against the glass. She swore that one of the guys from her IT class was drooling. "But if you really are from the zombie department, you must know how to fix this. Right?"

"I'm from the Department of Paranormal Containment, which means exactly that. We can't always stop it, but we can contain it."

Mia blinked. "I still don't have any idea what you're talking about. Isn't it the same thing?"

Chase shook his head and stood up just inches from where

she was standing. "No. *You* want to stop the virus before your friends all turn into zombies. I just want to stop the zombies from getting out into the greater area."

"A-and how do you intend on doing that?" Mia croaked.

"I have to kill them all." His voice was blunt and cold.

"Please tell me you're joking." Mia couldn't control the horror in her voice as Chase grimly shook his head.

"I'm not joking."

"But . . . you've got to be." She lowered herself back down onto the seat. "I mean, there must've been at least two hundred seniors at the assembly—"

"Not to mention teachers," he interjected.

"Right." Mia started to fan herself with her hand. There was a fair possibility that she might faint very soon. "Not to mention teachers."

"Killing them is the only way," he assured her, and Mia pressed her back against the table and stared at him.

"But that's ridiculous. There can't be any killing. What about Candice? I mean, sure, she's been having a binge-fest on beef jerky, but normally she's, like, a total white-meat girl. Plus, she's the only real friend I have. We're going to college together. I'm doing film studies, and she's doing pre-med. It's going to be our time to shine. How can we shine if she's a dead zombie with her head chopped off?"

"Who said anything about head chopping? We prefer more humane means. Like gas."

"Oh, well, that makes it all right then. Anyway, why are you even telling me this?" Mia demanded. "If you're so intent on killing everyone, why did you need me to know?"

Chase flushed and ran a hand through his short hair. "Actually, I probably shouldn't have done that—it's against protocol. It's just if I don't manage to deal with this virus properly and if even one infected zombie gets out, they'll head straight to you. I guess I just wanted to give you a heads-up so you could get out of here."

Mia shook her head. "I'm not going anywhere. Look, I watch a lot of TV and the one thing I've learned is that there's always a way. We just have to figure out what it is," she insisted. "When Samantha started flirting with Rob, did I just give up and let her get her false nails into him? No, I did something about it."

"Hence our problem," Chase pointed out.

"Okay, so perhaps that wasn't the best example. *But*," she continued, "there has to be a way to reverse this thing. I don't want everyone writing in my yearbook that I was the girl who turned them all into zombies. And what about the prom?"

"Zombies don't exactly have great motor skills. They can hardly hold up their heads, let alone write anything, so I think you're safe on that front," Chase informed her. "Though you might have problems filling your dance card."

She shot him a mutinous glare. "You're not funny."

"I'm not trying to be," he said in a grim voice, his face devoid of emotion. "Look, if I knew of another way, then I would've done it." He gripped his hands, and she couldn't help but notice his knuckles had turned white. "I don't like killing innocent people any more than you do."

"Well, obviously you do, since you were the one who suggested it in the first place." She folded her arms and glared at him, but his face remained impassive. "And it seems to me that you need to start learning to think outside the box."

"When the virus is still in stage one it's reversible," he repeated in a tight voice. "But once it reaches stage two, not only do I need the original incantation but also the person who did it, as well as the original ingredients that were in the spell."

"Well, there you go, Mr. Glass Half Empty," Mia said as a rush of relief raced through her. "It is reversible, after all. We've got the original incantation, and I was the one who did it, so now all we need are the ingredients."

"That's where the problem lies. It's impossible to ever find out the original ingredients."

"Really? Because I don't care if we have to strangle it out of her—if getting them will fix this thing, then I say we should do it."

"What?" Chase stared at her in astonishment.

"Oh please, you've got no problem with killing everyone, but you won't let me strangle some evil old hag who—"

"No, I mean, are you seriously saying you remember where you got the spell?"

"I paid a hundred bucks for it; I'm not likely to forget." She snorted before frowning. "Why?"

He rubbed his jaw in bewilderment. "Because normally when anyone does one of these, they suffer short-term memory loss. It's always built into the spell to protect the maker from being discovered. That's why we've never been able to reverse stage two before."

"Really?" Mia was surprised. "Maybe she has evil-old-witch dementia? Anyway, the important thing is that I totally remember everything about her. Her name is Algeria. She has a shop down at that old strip mall over by Moonlight Avenue, and she's about seven hundred and eighty-six years old with a squishy wrinkled face."

Chase pulled out his BlackBerry and typed in the information. "Ah, here we go. Algeria Chen. She's a low-level Chaos Maker."

"Do I even want to know what one of those is?" Mia shot him a dubious look.

"They sort of cause trouble on a freelance basis. She's probably been concocting and selling these spells for years on the off-chance that one of them might work." Chase looked up from the screen.

Mia frowned. "Yes, but what does she get out of it?"

"It's sort of like pyramid selling. The more zombies and other things her virus creates, the more . . . benefits . . . she gets from certain businessmen whose interests it suits to have the world in a state of . . . unrest."

"I never should've trusted her. You know, she had very beady eyes. So what are we waiting for?"

Chase paused for a minute and studied his BlackBerry. "According to this, her store doesn't open until eleven—"

"Even better. We can leave now and break in." Mia nodded her head in approval. "Then we can have this whole thing fixed before lunch. Perfect. Why are you shaking your head?"

"You think you can just break in and steal something from a Chaos Maker?" Chase lifted an eyebrow.

"Yes. Absolutely. Look," she wheedled, "I saw her use a black book to make the potion. She kept it in the top drawer behind her counter, and it had Elvis on the front of it. Can't we at least try to get it?"

"I've dealt with Chaos Makers before and you can't break in. The only way to gain entrance is if they invite you in or if the door is open. Which means we'll have to wait until she opens up for business."

"Oh, like vampires."

"I thought I told you that vampires don't exist." Chase frowned.

"I meant in *Buffy*," she explained. "If you're a vampire, you need to be invited in unless it's in a public place."

"Oh, right." Chase nodded. "Well, if they get hit by a thousand kilowatts of sonic energy by stepping over the threshold, then yeah, it's the same thing."

"We can get fried?" Mia gulped. Honestly, Algeria should come with a government health warning since she was getting nastier by the minute.

"Only if we try and break in. Look." Chase glanced at his

watch. "We might as well go to our class, and I'll meet you at the front of the school after second period. Okay?"

Mia nodded her head before she realized the seniors were still all lined up at the door. "Oh, and I don't suppose there is a way to lose this chicken smell? I think it might blow our cover if we have a group of almost-zombies trailing after us."

"There is something you can do, but I don't think you're going to like it."

Mia sighed. With the way the day was shaping up, that was a given.

seven

"It's water," Mia pronounced as she stood at Chase's locker and studied the spray bottle he had just given her. "I don't understand. Is it holy? Will it burn them?"

"You really do watch too much TV." He shook his head. "Actually, it's just tap water."

Mia looked at him blankly as she tried to ignore the gaggle of other seniors that had followed them and were now standing in a huddle on the other side of the hallway. Didn't these almost-zombies have classes to go to?

"You spray it on your skin," Chase explained. "Not only does it help buffer the pheromones you're putting out, but zombies hate water. Actually, if they're getting too close, you can just give them a quick squirt. It won't kill them or anything, but it will make them back off. I always keep a few bottles handy. Just in case."

"You want me to spray water all over myself?" She stared at

him as if he was nuts. Actually, scrap that. He was nuts. "I'll look like I'm trying out for a wet T-shirt contest."

"I said you wouldn't like it," Chase told her.

"Okay, fine. But if I find out this is some sort of zombie-hunter joke, I won't be happy," she informed him as she started to cautiously spray water on her exposed arms. A light mist settled onto her skin and the next minute the students started to disperse to their various classes.

"See?" He leaned against a nearby locker and lifted an eyebrow in her direction. "It works."

"So I don't smell like chicken anymore?" she checked.

"I don't have the zombie virus, so you never smelled like chicken to me," he assured her.

"Well, thanks. And sorry about the major freak-out. I still can't believe this is happening."

"I know. I'm sorry, too. When the department called to say a ritual had been done here at Newbury High, I thought they were joking. Then when they identified you as the person who did it, I definitely thought they were joking. I mean, you seem so normal."

"I *am* normal," Mia responded before letting out a sigh. "Well, I was. And then Rob asked me to the prom and Samantha started trying to steal him away and I just went a little . . . un-normal."

"I guess it happens. Though I wouldn't have thought Rob Ziggerman would be your type," he said, his green eyes drilling into her.

"What's that supposed to mean?" Mia bristled.

"Nothing." He shrugged and shook his head. "It's none of my business."

"That's right. And besides, he's totally my type." As she spoke, she tried not to notice how her damp skin prickled under Chase's gaze. She rubbed her arms to try and hide her reaction. It was obviously just from the water.

"If you say so." He reached over into his locker and pulled out two more bottles of water. "Anyway, until this thing is over, you'd better take these, as well."

"Thanks." Mia put them in her bag just as she caught sight of the inside of his locker, which was crammed with books and papers sticking out in all directions. A lot like her own. "Wow, it's messy."

"Oh, yeah. Don't ask me why but I can never keep it clean. I like to think of it as—"

"Organized chaos?" Mia suggested, and then grinned at him. "Me, too. I can't stand a neat locker. And it's good to see that you're not so perfect."

"Me? Perfect? What gave you that idea?" He looked at her in surprise.

"Well, you just seem like a rule-following zombie hunter, that's all." Mia shrugged. "I guess you didn't really strike me as a messy locker sort of guy."

"Looks can be deceiving," he said simply as he shut the door of his locker. As he did so, one of the many loose pieces of paper fluttered down to the ground. Mia bent down to pick it up and realized it was a photograph of a fragile-looking blonde-haired girl. She looked a little younger than Mia and was laughing at the camera, but unlike when Grace posed, there didn't seem to be any conceit or arrogance in the picture. Just sweetness.

Mia handed it back to him.

"That's Audrey," he said as he used his index finger to trace the image. "We went to school together in Boston."

"She's beautiful. Like *model* beautiful," Mia said, surprised to see how much his face softened as he looked at the photograph.

"Yeah." Chase's voice seemed distant and wistful. "She did some modeling when she was younger, but it wasn't really her thing. She was more about what was on the inside."

"You must miss her."

"I do," he said simply. "Every day."

"So will you move back to Boston to be closer to her when you graduate?" she asked as she studied his face to see his answer. It was weird that it made her look at him differently just because she knew he had a girlfriend. Chase's jaw tightened, but before he could open his mouth, there was a coughing noise from behind them.

"Chase Miller and Mia Everett. Is there any reason why you're still in the hallway instead of going to your next class?" a voice cut in, and they both spun around to where Principal Keegan was standing with an intrigued expression on his face. Crap. "By the way, Mia, this is for you." He held out a tube of Pringles and she let out a silent groan.

Double crap.

This day got worse by the minute. She quickly gave herself another spray of water as Chase shut his locker. Thankfully, Mr. Keegan suddenly dropped his hand back down to his side and looked confused.

"I'm sorry. I don't know what just came over me."

That would be the zombie virus I gave you. Mia gave herself another light squirt and just hoped she wouldn't have to smell like chicken for too much longer. Next to her, Chase was as still as a statue, and she had the crazy desire to reach out and touch his clenched fingers with her own.

"Anyway, I want you both to get to class right now. Understood?"

"Of course." Chase nodded as he gripped Mia's arm, and they both hurried away before the principal changed his mind.

"That was too close for comfort." She shivered and Chase pulled a sweatshirt out of his backpack.

"Here, put this on. You look cold," he said as he draped it over her shoulders. Mia was about to tell him she was fine, but the minute the faint lingering smell of soap that still clung to the fabric hit her nose, she found herself wrapping it around her arms.

"Thanks," she said as she tried to figure him out. He didn't seem to mind killing two hundred students, but he was worried about her catching a cold? And the worst of it was that despite knowing what he wanted to do, she felt safe around him. "So are you sure we have to wait until Algeria opens her shop?"

Chase nodded. "It's going to be hard enough as it is; we don't want to make it any more difficult than we need to. In the meantime, I think we should just go to our next classes, because the less attention we draw to ourselves, the better."

"And me sitting there spritzing myself every five minutes will look completely normal?" Mia raised an eyebrow.

"You're not in any immediate danger. The water is more to stop them annoying you than anything else."

"Okay, fine." Mia turned toward Business Studies. "So I'll see you out in the parking lot," she said as she watched him walk off down the hallway in long strides. Then she turned and gave herself one final light spray before she opened up the door, made her apologies for being late, and tried not to notice all the candy that was piled up on the desk where she normally sat. The sooner they got this sorted out, the better.

As Mia hurried out to the parking lot at ten thirty, she was relieved to see Chase was already there waiting for her. He was leaning against an old Impala that looked like it had seen better days. Still, the important thing was that he was on time, because even with her water spray, Mia's morning lessons had left her in no doubt that the zombie virus was real. Not only had people continued to give her food, but everyone around her seemed to be eating meat. Lots and lots of meat.

"Are you okay?" Chase asked as she hurried over to him.

"I'll be better when this is over. At this rate, no one is going to be able to fit into their prom dresses. Even Samantha Griffin, who has been on a permanent diet since she was eight, was eating a triple turkey-bacon sandwich."

"Let's just hope this works," Chase said as he walked around and opened her door. Wow, Mia didn't realize guys still did that sort of thing.

"It has to," she said in a firm voice as she hopped in.

Chase started the engine and pulled out onto Luna Drive. They made the short trip in silence and he soon pulled up at the strip mall, which didn't look any brighter or less dilapidated with a second viewing.

"You bought a spell from here and you didn't think it was weird?" He leaned across and opened her door from the inside.

"It seemed like a good idea at the time," Mia defended with a gulp as she got out of the car. It wasn't nearly as luxurious as Rob's SUV, but then again it probably had less chance of having its wheels stolen while they were away from it.

"Okay, so I suppose we should go and do this thing," Chase said. "But let me just remind you that Chaos Makers are very dangerous. In fact, it's probably best if you let me handle this."

As they walked through the door, Mia wrinkled her nose at the overwhelming smell of patchouli oil. She made a mental note that next time she smelled that, she would take it as a sign to turn around and leave.

"Hello, there. We have a lovely selection of virgin's blood on sale today." Algeria shuffled out from behind the beaded curtain; however, the moment she caught sight of Mia, her pale eyes narrowed. "Oh, it's you. No refunds if the spell didn't work."

"Yeah, well what about a refund if it turned everyone into zombies?" Mia demanded.

Algeria scoffed. "I have no idea what you're talking about," she said as she stepped back and fluttered her eyelashes, much the same way Grace did. It wasn't a good look on a fifteen-year-old girl, and it was even worse on an evil old bat. "Now, if you don't mind, I have work to do."

"Oh, like turning even more people into zombies?" Mia retorted as Chase glared at her.

"Remember our little chat outside?" he said through a clenched jaw. "Because you're really not helping matters."

"That's right. You should listen to your friend. I'm an honest businesswoman trying to make an honest living."

"Well, you might find that hard if all your stock is impounded by the Department of Paranormal Containment." Chase pulled out his BlackBerry and started to take pictures of the shop. "And my bosses will be especially interested to see that you have an Amstell 500 on the premises."

"It's good for cleaning crystals." The old woman gave a defensive shrug.

"It's also good for doing incarnations," he said as he walked straight past her behind the counter, where he began to inspect a large machine up on the top shelf. "And I'm going to need to see the license for that KS10 up here."

Mia glared at him. They were in the middle of a zombie crisis and he was worried about some stupid license for something that she'd never even heard of before?

"Fine," the old woman muttered. "It's in the back."

"Chase, what are you doing? Because this is not the time to be following the rule book," Mia hissed the minute the old woman had disappeared through the Elvis-beaded curtain.

"It's okay, I've got it," he assured her just as Algeria made her way back out and thrust a couple of pieces of paper at him.

"There. Like I said, I'm an honest businesswoman."

"Honest?" Mia spluttered as Chase glared at her some more. "You let me turn my whole class into zombies. How is that honest? Now tell us how to reverse it or else."

"Do I look like an amateur who would sell reversible rituals?" Algeria demanded as she waved an arthritic finger at her. "Pah. My rituals are foolproof."

"You are unbelievable." Mia clutched at the counter. "What kind of person would do that?"

"The kind who likes money," Algeria retorted. "And now I think it's time you leave. I've got wards set all over this place and if you cause me any violence or distress, let's just say it won't bode well for you."

Okay, this was not good news.

Especially since Algeria's finger had gone a glowy red color, and while Mia had no idea what a ward was, since the woman was capable of selling innocent teenage girls zombie spells, she was probably capable of anything.

She took a wobbly step back from the old woman and looked over to Chase for any ideas. "So what does the department recommend in situations like this?"

"Running," Chase replied as he grabbed her hand and quickly headed for the door. "Whenever a Chaos Maker threatens physical harm, the department is a big fan of running."

They darted out of the store and came to a puffing halt by Chase's car.

"Oh, God. That woman is crazy. Did you see her eyes? And her finger looked like it was going to start zapping sparks." Mia leaned against the Impala. "On the other hand, we're back to square one. Are you sure we shouldn't have just tried to attack her? I mean, how much would one of those ward things really hurt?"

"A lot," Chase assured her as he pulled a small black book out of his pocket and waved it in the air. "And anyway, I thought I told you that I had it."

Mia widened her eyes at the sight of the velvet-covered book. "*You got it?* I thought you meant you had it under control; I didn't realize you were being literal. How did you even get it?"

Chase shot her a rare smile and she realized he had dimples. Huh. He should smile more often—it suited him.

"So where to now? What ingredients do we need? Because the sooner this is over with the . . . Why do you have your serious face on again?" Mia demanded as she realized Chase was no longer smiling. In fact, he looked downright grim as he quickly started to flip through the book.

"We have a problem," he said.

"Yes, I know," she agreed. "Two hundred zombie students. But—"

"No." He cut her off with a shake of his head. "We have a new problem. This entire book is written in Latin."

"Latin?" Mia wrinkled her nose and studied the pages. "Why would it be in Latin?"

"To stop department agents like myself from translating it, I guess." Chase shrugged. "And if that was the plan, then it's definitely worked since my Latin is a little rusty. Actually, it's nonexistent. I'm sorry, Mia, I really thought we had a chance to—"

"Don't say it." She shook her head. "Don't even think it."

"Mia, this book has over a hundred pages, and I don't even know where the right spell is, let alone how to translate it."

"Well, what about your department?"

He shook his head and frowned. "We just don't have the resources. Especially if the virus is going to hit stage four tomorrow."

"What do you mean you don't have the resources? What sort of place is it?"

"Strangely enough, not everyone wants to fight paranormal creatures. Recruitment is an issue. As is funding. I promise you I'm not trying to be difficult, and if there was any other way I—"

"Candice!" Mia suddenly turned to him. "That's it."

"Look." Chase reached out and squeezed her hand in what she guessed was a standard zombie-hunter manner when a civilian was about to have a freak-out. "I know how much you want to save your friend, but—"

"No, I don't mean that. I mean that Candice could help us."

"Why, can she speak Latin?"

"Yes, actually, she can," Mia informed him before amending. "Well, she can read it anyway. Apparently loads of medical jargon is still in Latin. Do you know what St. Anthony's fire is?"

"No." He shook his head and looked perplexed.

"Well, I didn't either, but apparently it's some medieval disease," Mia confessed. "The thing is, Candice thought she had it, and she totally found out how to cure it, but it was all written in Latin, so guess what? She translated it. Of course, in the end, it was because her new bra was too tight for her and it was crushing her chest and making her feel faint, but that's not the point. The point is that when it comes to Latin, she knows her stuff. Please, Chase, can you just put the rule book away for a minute and let us at least try?"

For a moment he frowned before merely reaching down and opening up the passenger-side door of the Impala. "Fine, let's just hope she really is as good as you say she is."

eight

"*I*'m a *what?*" Candice spluttered into her Diet Coke.

"Keep your voice down," Mia warned as she glanced around the cafeteria where she had finally found her friend and tried not to notice how busy it was. Especially since the food was so diabolically bad that it was normally half empty. Either the students wanted to be near her or they wanted to eat the gross, fatty burgers. Right now Mia didn't quite know which was worse. At least she had convinced Chase to let her talk to Candice alone, since it was difficult to say just how her friend would take the news.

"Keep my voice down?" her friend screeched. "How do you expect me to do that when you've just told me I'm a zombie?"

Okay, so she wasn't taking it well. Though to be fair, neither had Mia, so she couldn't really hold it against her.

"I know it's a lot to take in, and seriously I can't begin to tell you how sorry I am that it's happened, but I'm afraid it's true. You're turning into a zombie," Mia said as Candice put down the rest of her drink and held her hands up to her eyes.

"Oh, this is bad." Candice moaned in a loud voice. "So bad. I can't believe how bad this is. Do you know how it feels to have a life-threatening disease? I mean, I could die."

"But you think you have a life-threatening disease every week," Mia reminded her friend, but Candice waved it off.

"Oh, puh-*lease*. I knew those things weren't real, but this? Oh my God, I'm going to die," her friend continued to lament, and a few people looked over.

"Candice. *Candice*," Mia repeated, this time shaking her arm. "You're not going to die, because . . . Oh my God. Gross. *Did you just lick my fingers?*"

"Sorry." Her friend broke off from her wailing for a moment and thoughtfully ran her tongue around her lips as if to savor the taste. "I think it's the disease. It's taking over my body. I can't control it."

"Well, you'd better control it," Mia retorted as she wiped her fingers on a napkin. "Because that was the most disgusting thing. Ever. No more finger licking."

"Okay, so tell me the worst. How much longer do I have?"

"Until tomorrow at lunchtime." Mia winced. "Look, I can't begin to imagine how hard this must be, but—"

"Hard? It's more than hard, it's . . . Hang on a minute." Candice suddenly looked up and narrowed her eyes. "Why can't you imagine what it's like? You were the one who did the spell, so you must be a turning into a bone-munching brain-sucker, too."

"Apparently the brain-sucking thing is a myth," Mia explained before gulping. "And it turns out that because I did the spell, I'm sort of immune to the virus. Instead I've become the queen."

"Oh, you've got to be kidding me." Candice shot her a dangerous glare. "Are you telling me that I get to be turned into a zombie and you get to be queen?"

"Yeah, it's just great being queen. I'm having so much fun that it's unbelievable." Mia folded her arms as the events of the morning unraveled in her mind. "I turn you all into zombies, and in return you guys love me so much that you want to make me get really fat so that you can *eat me*."

"Oh." Candice looked a bit appeased. "Well, I guess as long as you didn't get off scot-free, it's okay. Anyway, how do you know all this stuff? Don't tell me there is a hidden *Buffy* episode that I missed?"

Mia shook her head. "Actually, it's Chase Miller. Would you believe he's a zombie hunter?"

Candice looked surprised. "New Boy? Wow, I never saw that one coming. Talk about hidden depths. Cute and committed."

"I don't know why you keep saying he's cute. I mean, I guess he's okay. But don't you think he's too tall? Not to mention serious. Oh, and he likes to do everything by the book."

"Works for me. So how come he didn't get the virus?"

"He's immune to the disease, too. Apparently he's got some sort of mutant gene. It's hereditary."

"Oh, did he say what kind?" Candice was momentarily distracted as she looked up with interest.

"I'm guessing the mutant kind," Mia answered before pulling the black book out of her bag. "But in the meantime, if we can forget about Chase and his genes, we've got to concentrate so we can get the cure for this thing so no one has to die."

"*There's a cure?*" Candice straightened her spine and shot her a reproachful glance. "Why didn't you say so right at the beginning? Sheesh, Mia, next time this happens, try giving me the good news first, please."

"Okay, so first up, there isn't going to be a next time, and when I said there's a cure, the thing is that *technically* no one has ever done it before," Mia was forced to admit. "The problem is, we need to get a list of the ingredients from the original spell but the book we stole from Algeria is all written in Latin."

"You stole her book? I'm not sure that's very wise. She needs that book to work her magic."

"Candice, her magic turned you into a Z-O-M-B-I-E," Mia reminded her friend in a low voice before passing over the book. "Anyway, if you could translate it for us, then we might have a chance of fixing this thing."

"Let me see that." Candice suddenly pushed away the remains of her lunch and cleared the table space in front of her.

"Well?" Mia caught her breath as Candice continued to study it before finally looking up.

"This might take a while but I'm pretty sure I can do it."

"You can?" Mia felt a surge of relief flow through her. "That's great. What can I do to help?"

"You can go and get me another burger. Oh, and hold the bread. And the cheese . . ."

"Are these people insane?" Mia demanded fifteen minutes later as yet another student came up and gave her food. This time it was a packet of M&Ms and she looked at the growing pile in the middle of the table. How they thought she was going to eat all this stuff was anyone's guess. Next to her, Chase, who had joined them not long after Candice had started working on the translation, glanced around and frowned.

"What's wrong?" she demanded. "You're not thinking of doing anything *gassy* are you?"

"You make it sound like I *want* to kill these people." Chase looked offended. "Trust me, I hope just as much as you do that this reversal works. But if it doesn't, then—"

"I know. You need to follow procedure and do your job." Mia sighed as she unconsciously ripped the M&Ms open and popped a red one into her mouth.

For a moment Chase clenched his jaw before nodding. "Well, I'm glad you understand. Anyway, have you noticed how many seniors are in here? And they're all eating a lot of meat."

Mia stood up and peered around. Chase was right. She

pulled out her spray bottle and gave herself another squirt. Two seconds later, about fifty seniors all stood up and pretended to squirt themselves.

"Did you see that?" she demanded. "First they want to eat me and now they want to mock me, too?"

"It's their duty to follow you as much as possible," Chase explained.

"Until it's time for dinner," Mia reminded him as she looked over her shoulder. All the seniors in the room followed suit. Great, zombie lemmings. Perhaps she should just lead them all over the edge of a cliff? Apart from the fact that she wasn't exactly a fan of heights. Or cliff jumping, for that matter. She ate some more candy.

"*Carno. Carn. Carni,*" Candice muttered before glancing up and grinning. Mia tried to ignore the bits of meat that were stuck in her friend's teeth. "Oh hey, Chase, I didn't see you there. I really like that shirt."

Mia blinked. Was Candice flirting? In the middle of a zombie crisis?

"Er, thanks." He flushed and studied his fingers.

"Yeah, it really brings out the green in your eyes and . . . What? Why are you looking at me like that, Mia?"

"Because the sooner we get this reversal spell done, the sooner things can go back to normal. So how's it going?"

Candice frowned. "She has some awesome spells in here. There is one that lets you turn your entire family into slugs. I mean, that's just plain mean."

"What about the *Viral Zombaticus*?" Chase looked concerned. "Have you managed to find that yet?"

"Yup, it was right in the middle of the book. She even had a little scary face drawn on it." Candice held up the book before catching their expressions. "Okay, fine, I'll start translating the ingredients," she muttered as she turned her attention back to her Latin books. Mia nodded for Chase to follow her over to the next table so they wouldn't disturb her anymore.

"You're doing a good job of holding it together," he said unexpectedly.

Mia looked at him in surprise. She wondered if that was in the handbook under "How to Calm Freaked-Out Zombie Queens."

"Thanks. So, how did you even get into this business?" she asked as she passed over the M&Ms, and he helped himself to a couple of blue ones. For a moment he paused and studied the candy before finally looking back up at her, his green eyes meeting hers.

"When I was fifteen, the school I went to in Boston had a zombie outbreak. But because I was immune, I didn't get turned, and somehow I managed to get out of there without becoming someone's eleven o'clock snack."

"Oh my God. What happened to everyone else?"

"By the time the department had finished containing it, there was only one person left. Me."

Mia looked at him blankly for a moment. "But I don't understand—if no one was left, what about Audrey? I'm sure you said you both went to school together, so how did she—"

"Escape the virus?" Chase finished off before shaking his head and not quite meeting her gaze. "She didn't. Audrey got infected just like everyone else."

"Oh," Mia said inadequately. Audrey was a zombie? Well, she hadn't seen that one coming.

"I tried to save her." His voice was tight and his face curiously devoid of emotion. "I thought if I could just keep her safe that we would find a cure. I'd known her since we were eight. We grew up together. I figured there had to be a way."

"So what happened?" Mia's voice wasn't much more than a whisper, but Chase shook his head.

"Someone from the department killed her just in time." He held out his arm and lifted his shirt sleeve to reveal a long red scar that ran all the way up his forearm.

She sucked in her breath. "I truly had no idea. I just saw your face when you were telling me about her and thought you were still—"

"It's okay. It's been a long time since I've really talked about her; it was actually easier than it used to be."

"So what happened after that?" Mia could hardly bring herself to ask.

"The department tested me to see why I had survived and when they discovered my immunity, they stopped trying to cover it up and recruited me to help out when I could. On a part-time basis, of course, because my folks refused to let me drop out of school."

"You've been doing this part-time since you were fifteen?" When Mia was fifteen, she had been fighting with Candice over who loved Adam Brody more. Come to think of it, they still did that now. "But what about the other things you wanted to do with your life?"

"There were eight hundred kids at my old school and three days later there was only one," he simply said. "It's not something you can turn your back on. It's not something I *want* to turn my back on."

She felt her eyes mist up as she stared at him. For six months he had been at their school, sitting at the back of the class just acting like a regular kid—well, a regular kid who kept to himself and didn't seem to mind being called New Boy. But really, the whole time he had been living this secret life. A secret life full of zombies and death. No wonder he didn't bother much with the small talk, since most things must seem a bit inane compared to what he had been through. Mia studied his face. His normal controlled expression was gone and in its place was one of hurt and pain.

Suddenly his desire to do everything by the rule book made a little bit more sense.

"Chase, I didn't realize—"

"Now, *that's* what I'm talking about." Candice suddenly stood up and made a stirring motion with her hands in a little victory dance. For a moment Mia just blinked before realizing her friend must've found something.

"What do you have?" Chase hurried over.

"Only the list of ingredients." Candice grinned. "Though you know, to be honest, it looks more like a grocery list. Basil, vanilla essence, jasmine, rock salt, mandrake root, four coffin nails—okay, you might have to go somewhere else for those last two. Anyway, here it is." She passed it to Chase, and Mia started to clap.

"Candice, you're a genius."

"I've often thought so." Her friend reached out and shoved the rest of her discarded burger into her mouth and grinned as Chase studied the list.

"So? What do you think? Can we get all this stuff?" Mia asked and didn't realize she was holding her breath until he nodded his head.

"There's a specialist supplier just outside of town. I've been there a couple of times and he should have everything we need."

"And he's not a Chaos Maker?" Mia double-checked. Never let it be said she didn't learn a lesson.

"Definitely not." He got to his feet and put the list in his pocket. "I'll head over there now and then we can get to work."

"Okay, thanks, Chase." Mia shot him a grateful look as he gave Candice a quick nod and hurried out of the cafeteria.

"You know, the more I look at the guy, the cuter he

becomes," Candice announced once Chase had moved out of hearing. "I wonder if he's going to the prom?"

"I doubt it. He just doesn't look like the prom sort of person."

"Well, all the same, I might ask him. After all, I did buy a second prom ticket so that my future boyfriend would know I was ready for him."

"What?" Mia blinked at her friend. "Are you serious?"

"Sure, why not?" Candice shrugged. "He obviously thinks I'm smart since I translated Latin. Hey, maybe I could end up being his partner in crime? We could wear matching outfits."

"Candice, we're in the middle of a zombie crisis. How can you even think about the prom? Besides, what if you go all carnivore and try and eat him?"

"I'm pretty sure I wouldn't," Candice protested. "Anyway, why are you so upset? It's *your* prom obsession that got us into this mess in the first place, and once we're all saved, you'll be going with Rob. Besides, don't you think it's amazing how Chase is so determined to save us?"

"Determined? He wanted to follow the rules and kill you all. With gas. But I was the one who wouldn't let him."

"You know, Mia, you're acting very defensive about this." Candice blinked. "I thought you'd be happy if I went with someone since it will stop me crowding you and Rob so much. Oh, and speak of the devil," Candice said, and Mia looked up to see Rob jogging toward the table holding an overflowing tray of food. Before he arrived, Mia quickly grabbed Algeria's book and tucked it safely away in her bag. No good could come from anyone seeing it.

"Mia, there you are. I'm glad I found you. It's been such a crazy day. First someone hit my SUV and dented the fender, which is a total pain because it's custom made. And then I find out I might be benched for the next football game. Something about a bad science grade." He shook his head.

Mia only just resisted the urge to burst out laughing since Rob's day sounded pretty much perfect compared to her own. But before she could say anything, he looked at her with interest.

"Hey, have you been eating chicken? Something smells great around here."

Mia gulped. She looked down and couldn't help but notice that Rob's left arm was uncontrollably twitching by his side.

Chase had better hurry up with that list. Like, seriously.

nine

"Thank God school's over for the day," Mia said to Candice as she hurried out of class and down the front stairs of Newbury High the second the final bell rang. Chase had sent her a text to say he would meet them in the parking lot.

"Why? Did *you* feel the need to eat five hamburgers in a row and then wonder if they'd taste better uncooked?" Candice retorted sarcastically as she fished out her car keys.

"Okay, so perhaps your day was bad, too. But at least you didn't have zombies stalking you—no offense. I'm still glad it's over," she conceded as she realized Candice was still a bit pissed at her. Funny that her friend didn't mind Mia had accidently turned her into a zombie, but she didn't seem to like being told that asking Chase Miller to the prom was a bad idea.

But before she could say anything else, her math teacher walked past and gave her an appreciative sniff. Mia shuddered. According to her count, so far she'd managed to turn five teachers into almost-zombies. She pulled out her water bottle and gave herself another squirt as Candice shot her a wide-eyed stare.

"Why exactly are you spraying yourself with water?"

"To stop me smelling like chicken, of course. Didn't you just see how Mrs. Walcott was looking at me? I swear she could picture a gravy boat floating just above my head. It's creeping me out."

"Chicken? You don't smell like chicken. You smell like someone who ate an overcooked burrito for lunch, but definitely not like any poultry."

"Really?" Mia held up her arm to Candice's nose. "So when I do this, you really don't feel like eating me?"

Candice wrinkled her nose in distaste. "Hardly. A little lick maybe, but no chewing. You know, I have enough problems with my sensitive stomach as it is. Actually, that reminds me—I should take my antacids." She pulled a small bottle out of her bag and shook out a couple of tablets. For a moment Mia just stared at her friend with interest, but before she could say anything, Rob came out of the building and started to eagerly glance around.

"Get down here." She tugged at her friend's sleeve and tried to pull her down behind the VW.

"What?" Candice stared down at her. "I'm not getting down there. You know what my knees are like. Is this some sort of zombie-queen thing?"

"Candice, please just do it," Mia let out an urgent hiss

as Rob continued to look around the parking lot. The main problem that came from hanging out with the same person for the last zillion years was that most people knew if they found one of them, the other wasn't too far behind.

"Fine." Candice grudgingly dropped down and peered around. "But what's this about? Oh, hey, isn't that Rob over there? It seems like he's looking for you. Once this whole zombie business is sorted out, you really need to get your eyes tested."

"My eyesight is just fine, thank you very much," she said.

"Well, maybe it's your brain that's malfunctioning then, because why are we hiding when it's obvious he wants to find you? I mean, this whole situation is because of him."

Yes. Mia gulped. *So it was.*

As she watched Rob's left arm continue to twitch uncontrollably, she couldn't help but think of the eight burgers he had devoured in the cafeteria. And why had she never noticed how pointy his teeth were before? Not that she was going to tell Candice that. Or Rob, for that matter. Hiding was a much better option, at least until they had done the reversal spell. Her membership card for the Spineless Wonder Club should be arriving in the mail any day now.

"Well?" Candice shot her a quizzing glare. "What's going on?"

"Nothing," Mia assured her. "It's just with this whole zombie business, it would hardly be appropriate for me to just go off with Rob. I need to stay focused."

"Are you sure?"

"Of course—" Mia started to assure her just as Samantha suddenly stormed up to them.

"Mia, there you are," the cheerleader said in a particularly loud voice, which in turn meant that not only Rob but half a dozen other seniors all started to walk slowly toward them.

"Hey, Samantha." Mia got to her feet and started to edge back toward Candice. "S-so what can I do for you?"

"You can tell me why you are so determined to ruin my life," Samantha snapped. "Because all I've heard today is *Mia this, Mia that, Mia, freaking Mia*. Well, let me tell you, I've dreamed of being prom queen since I was a little girl, and if you think I'm going to let some *Buffy*-obsessed nobody come along and take it all away from me, you're wrong."

"You know, she looks pretty pissed off," Candice warned in a low voice as Rob and the rest of the seniors joined Samantha and started to press in on them. All that was missing was the "You're going to die, losers," horror music and the picture would've been complete.

"Get in," a voice called out, and Mia and Candice both spun around to see Chase's Impala screeching to a halt next to them. Never had she been so happy to see anyone. Mia tried to ignore her shaking hands as she pulled out her water bottle and gave Samantha and the rest of them a squirt of water before gratefully jumping into Chase's car.

"Oh my God. What is wrong with them?" Candice scrambled into the backseat and slammed the door shut.

"It's the virus," Chase explained as he drove off, leaving Samantha and the others standing in the parking lot looking perplexed. "As it progresses through stage two, the cravings start to increase. As does the loss of motor functions. Were any of them twitching?"

"Yes," Mia took a deep breath and tried to collect herself. "So would they have tried to hurt me?"

"I don't think so." Chase shook his head. "They were probably just as freaked out as you were."

"I doubt that," Mia assured him. Then she frowned as she turned to where Candice was sitting in the backseat opening up a small bottle.

"It's Rescue Remedy," her friend explained as she held it up. "It's good for stress, and if that situation back there wasn't stressful, then I don't know what is. Do you want some?"

"Er, no thanks," Mia said before turning to Chase. "This loss of motor skills? Does it include opening bottles?"

"Sure, I guess." He shrugged. "Why?"

"Well, isn't it a bit weird that Candice didn't go all zombie along with the others back there? And that reminds me, she doesn't seem to think I smell like chicken, either."

"Are you sure she's not just being nice to you?" He lifted an eyebrow but Mia shook her head.

"You obviously don't know Candice very well. She calls it like she sees it. Anyway, she said I don't smell."

"I said you don't smell like chicken," Candice corrected from the backseat. "So what does it mean? Maybe this whole zombie thing isn't as bad as we thought? I could even be immune like you guys. I mean, I was right next to Mia when she did the spell."

"Normally there's only one queen." Chase chewed on his bottom lip as he pulled the Impala over to the side of the road and turned to study Candice's face. "I'm afraid not. See the way the skin is starting to go slack around the eyes and mouth? That's definitely a sign of stage two, but it does seem like something in her body is slowing down the virus," he said thoughtfully as they both watched Candice put her bottle of Rescue Remedy back into her purse.

"What?" Candice demanded. "Why are you both looking at me like that?"

"Do you think it's because of all the vitamins she takes?" Mia asked. "I mean, her phone beeps at least ten times a day to remind her to take things. She's a walking pharmacy."

"I have no idea what it means, but it might be handy to know," Chase conceded.

"Well, I'm pleased you're both so happy about it," Candice muttered as she touched her eyes and mouth to no doubt check for sagging skin.

"No one is happy," Mia assured her friend as Chase started up the engine again. "So what happens now? Did you get all the ingredients?"

"I did, so we just need to mix it all up and then wait until tomorrow."

"Tomorrow?" Candice protested. "That's a long way off,

and who knows what sort of irreparable damage this is doing to my body. Plus, I have serious doubts that my parents' medical insurance will cover my zombie-rehabilitation expenses."

"We still have some time before the virus moves into stage three," Chase promised. "And we need to do it at school so that we don't miss anyone. We just have to hope that no one is out sick."

Mia gave an adamant nod of her head. "No complaints from me, and if you want, we can go back to my house to do it. Grace has cheerleading practice and my mom works late on Wednesdays."

"Actually, if you don't need me I might just go straight home," Candice said as she smothered a yawn. "I think all of that protein is starting to make me tired."

"Sure," Chase said as they headed up Crescent Grove to the nicer part of the Twilight Zone, where all the houses looked like they had been supersized with long driveways and *Gone with the Wind*–style pillars at the front. Candice's was the most supersized of them all.

"Thanks for the lift," Candice said as Chase leaned into the backseat and opened the door for her. Mia noticed her friend's face was pale and strained.

"That's okay," Chase said. "And since your car's still at school, I'll come by and pick you up in the morning if you want."

"You will?"

"Of course," he said as he gave her a double-dimpled smile.

"And Candice, try not to panic. Now that we've got all the ingredients and the full incantation, there's no reason why the reversal shouldn't work. So don't be thinking you're dying. Okay?"

"Okay." Candice managed a nod, but it wasn't until she had disappeared up the path and into the enormous house that Mia turned to him in surprise.

"That was really sweet of you."

"It's nothing. It can't be easy for her. The rest of the people who are infected probably don't even realize it, but since Candice is aware of what is happening, not to mention seems concerned about her health, I just didn't want her to worry."

"Well, it was still very nice of you. Not everyone gets Candice. Her dad is a financial wizard and her mom works in real estate selling massive condos. They have more bathrooms than we have bedrooms. Problem is her folks work so hard that they're hardly ever at home. That's why she's a bit of a hypochondriac. She had the flu when she was about eight and her mom took the day off to stay with her. I think she's been trying to replicate it ever since."

"Well, turning into a zombie would certainly get their attention. Though probably not in a good way," Chase said as he started the engine to make the short drive to her own house. As he drove, Mia couldn't help but study him.

There was definitely more to Chase Miller than met the eye. Not that she'd met any other zombie hunters before, but she wouldn't have expected them to be so kind or so calm under pressure. She started to understand that part of the reason she hadn't succumbed to a complete meltdown was because of Chase's soothing presence. For a moment she wondered what Rob would be like under the circumstances, but she realized that was just futile since it was never going to happen. Besides, Rob was kind as well. Maybe a bit more self-centered than Chase, but he wasn't purposefully cruel like Samantha and most of the other popular group. And anyway—

"Are you okay?" Chase suddenly asked, and Mia realized she had been staring at him the whole time.

"Oh, right." She flushed as he turned right at the end of the leafy street and headed down Moonshine Drive. "Yeah, I'm fine. Well, as fine as I can be, I guess," she said, and wondered if he'd try and reassure her like he'd done with Candice—maybe use his dimples. But he just shrugged, and once he pulled up outside her house, he turned to her.

"So, are you sure it's okay to do this here? I don't want to get you in trouble."

"I think I've managed that all on my own. Anyway, it's fine," she assured him as he once again reached across her and opened her door. This time Mia was aware that his arm grazed hers. She jumped slightly and got out of the car. This zombie business was obviously affecting her nerves. Chase walked around to the trunk and pulled out a large brown bag and they both hurried inside.

"My room's upstairs." She nodded for him to follow her up, but it wasn't until he stepped in that she realized how odd it was to be spending so much time with a guy who two days ago she probably wouldn't have been able to pick out in a lineup.

"Wow, you really do like *Buffy* and *Angel*." Chase put the bag down on her bed and looked around at the numerous posters that were plastered all over the wall. Suddenly she felt like a twelve-year-old girl as she caught sight of all the clothes that were scattered around the place.

"You probably think it's dumb," she said as she started to scoop them all up. Next to the bed was one of Grace's magazines that Mia had been secretly looking at to figure out how to do her hair for Friday. She used her foot to kick it out of sight.

"Why? Because I know that vampires don't really exist?" he teased, and Mia felt her eyes widen as she thrust all the clothes into her closet.

"Did you just make a joke?"

"Yes, but don't tell anyone or else they will kick me out of the zombie hunters' club."

"That was another joke," she pointed out as she caught sight of all her DVDs strewn across the floor by the window. She darted over but he stepped in front of her.

"Mia, you don't need to clean up for me. I thought we'd both established that organized chaos was okay. Besides, we're only here to mix this stuff together. And speaking of which, we should probably get started."

"Oh, right. Of course," Mia agreed. Besides, it wasn't like she cared what Chase Miller thought of her room. More to the point, judging from his reaction, he didn't care, either. He was just doing his job. Though she should probably remember that if Rob ever came up to her room, then she would definitely need to clean up since it appeared he was a bit of a neat freak.

"So, according to Candice's translation, it's a pretty standard mixture, though since I don't make them as often as Algeria probably does, it might take a bit longer."

"As long as it works, that's okay," Mia assured him as she cleared some space on the floor and Chase started to pull out bottle after bottle of ingredients. Then he set up a large mortar and pestle and flattened out Candice's instructions.

"Right," he said. "If you can read it out loud to me, I'll get to work."

"Okay, two teaspoons of rock salt. But it needs to be ground not crushed."

"Ground rock salt coming up." Chase opened a bottle and carefully measured it out before glancing back up to her for the next ingredient. Mia grinned as she continued to read, all the time watching as his steady hands mixed and measured. If she was doing it, it probably would've turned out into a soggy mess like when she'd been forced to make muffins in home economics, but she got the feeling that Chase never made mistakes like that. Even under duress he seemed cool, calm, and collected. No wonder he was such a good zombie hunter.

Finally he looked up at her as he gave it one last stir. "Okay, it's done," he said as he started to put lids back on all the bottles. Mia didn't know whether to be relieved or a little concerned at just how easy it all appeared to be.

"So what now?"

"Now we need to figure out the best place to do the spell. We want everyone to be in one place." As he spoke, he stood up and stretched his legs just as there was a noise from out in the hallway. Mia instantly jumped to her feet and grabbed her water bottle before glancing at Chase.

"You don't think it's—"

"Technically it shouldn't be," Chase said in a low voice, but all the same he nodded for her to stay where she was. No problem there, since her feet didn't feel capable of moving, and she watched as he inched his way to the door. Mia's heart started to pound as the sound of footsteps in the hallway got louder. It almost sounded like someone was racing toward them. Did zombies race? She had a feeling they didn't, but then again, what did she know?

And not for the first time she felt the panic start to rise in her chest. This was real. She had turned everyone into zombies. Zombies that wanted to eat her. She used her hand to try and fan down her face before Chase could realize just how terrified she was.

The footsteps were getting closer now, and Mia slunk farther back toward the bed. She glanced over to where Chase was flat against the wall next to the door and he was holding some sort of metal-looking baton high above his head. Then, before she knew what was happening, the door flew open and a deranged creature charged toward her.

ten

"*Grace?*" Mia shouted in surprise as she realized the deranged creature was in fact just her sister (whose face was, to be fair, a mask of fury). In an instant, Chase lowered his arm and slipped out of the room into the hallway and Mia shot him a grateful smile since right now she wasn't up to explaining what they had been doing.

"Don't you 'Grace' me," her sister snapped as she came to a halt in the center of the room and folded her arms. "I can't believe you made people nominate you for prom queen."

"Of course I didn't make anyone nominate me," Mia retorted as she tried to gather her frayed nerves. *I merely turned them into zombies and made myself the top of their food chain. There's a big difference.*

"Oh, really." Grace narrowed her lips. "And you're trying to tell me that it happened because people like you?"

Again, that would be down to the zombie virus that I infected them all with. Keep up.

"Yes," Mia said instead.

"Well, you might be able to fool everyone else, but you can't fool me. I know exactly how you managed it."

"You do?" This time Mia felt a surge of alarm go racing through her. Grace didn't look like the sharpest knife in the drawer, but she had supersonic hearing that would make the Bionic Woman proud. Somehow she must've overheard Mia talking to Chase about it. Why hadn't Mia double-checked that her sister wasn't home instead of just assuming she was at cheerleading practice?

"Yes, and I've got to say that it's pathetic," Grace said as she stared directly at the numerous bottles and the bowl of zombie potion sitting on the floor in the middle of her bedroom.

"Look," she said, "it's not all my fault. If Samantha hadn't tried to steal my prom date then none of this would've happened."

"At least Samantha has the dignity to run an honest campaign, but apparently you've been spraying water on yourself like some Playboy Bunny. What I don't get is how on earth you thought that would get you any votes?" Grace demanded.

Mia glanced down at Chase's sweatshirt, which was still a little damp, before looking up at her sister again. "So you think that's why people want to vote for me?" she double-checked.

"Well, duh." Grace rolled her eyes. "Anyway, Samantha is really upset. Unfortunately, we've already checked with the office, and you're not allowed to withdraw."

"Withdraw?" Mia shot her sister a blank look. Thanks to the whole zombie crisis, she really hadn't given too much thought about her prom-queen nomination in the first place. Well, she had, but her initial excitement had quickly been curtailed when she had found out just *why* she had suddenly become so popular.

"I said you're not allowed to withdraw," Grace repeated as if she were speaking to a six-year-old. "But you'd better not do anything embarrassing at your speech tomorrow—"

"Speech? What speech?"

"You see, this is the reason you don't deserve to even be on the ballot in the first place." Grace waved her arm in the air in disgust before once again adopting her know-it-all voice. "At your senior assembly tomorrow, all the nominees get to do a five-minute speech on why people should vote for them. And I'm warning you—"

"Enough." Mia marched over and started to guide her back toward the door. "I don't need my fifteen-year-old sister telling me what to do. Now, if you don't mind, I've got more important things to worry about."

"You are so pathetic," Grace muttered before turning and marching off.

A moment later, Chase slipped back into her room, obviously undetected by Grace. Mia shook her head in annoyance. "Man, what is she so upset about? I mean, why is it so unbelievable that I've been nominated for prom queen? Well, okay, so perhaps I did use the forces of darkness to make it happen, but that's beside the point. The point is that I've got a good mind to do a speech just to annoy her and Samantha Griffin."

"I don't think that's a good idea." Chase shook his head, and Mia looked at him in surprise.

"What? How hard could it be? And it's not that I asked to be nominated, but it's a bit insulting that Grace doesn't think I can—"

"Mia, that's not what I meant. It's just that we both forgot about the other senior-class assembly. That's when we can do the reversal spell."

"Oh." Mia widened her eyes in understanding. "You're right. It's perfect. Anyway, it's probably for the best since I was lying about the speech thing being easy. I probably would've been terrible, and I wouldn't have a clue what to say."

"I'm sure you would've worked something out." Chase shrugged as he started to gather everything up before carefully pouring the potion into a spare bottle. Once he was finished, he held it out to her. "So do you want to take this or should I?"

"You," she automatically said, since with the way her luck had been lately, it was odds on that she would break it.

"Sure." He shrugged as he stood back and prepared to leave. "So I'd better get going, but if you'd like, I'll pick you up tomorrow after I get Candice."

"Thanks," Mia said as she poked her head out of the door

to check that Grace was nowhere around before nodding for him to follow her down the stairs.

"And look, if you're worried about anything happening tonight, don't be. The virus is still definitely in stage two, so even if someone wanted to eat you, they probably couldn't manage it. Their teeth and their bile glands aren't fully developed yet." Then he groaned. "Did I really just say that out loud?"

"It's okay, I know what you meant," she assured him as she realized that he had seen how scared she was back in the room. Then he shot her a rueful grin that transformed his face, and suddenly Mia could understand what Audrey had seen in him. And Candice, for that matter.

"Cool. So, I'll see you tomorrow then. Oh, and Mia, I like your prom dress."

Huh? She paused for a moment before recalling that her dress had been hanging on the outside of her closet. But Chase was already opening the door to his Impala. She waved goodbye before heading back inside and trying to think how much better it would be this time tomorrow, when no one wanted to eat her anymore.

"Mia, why didn't you tell me?" her mom asked the next morning.

Mia looked up from the cereal that she had been pushing around her bowl. "T-tell you what?" She tried to plaster a bright smile onto her sleep-deprived face so that she didn't look like the girl who had stayed up most of the night worrying about the zombies she had accidently created.

At first she had just worried about getting her chanting right, but as the night had worn on, she'd started to worry that Candice and the others had ended up turning all carnivore and had eaten everyone in Newbury (Chase included) and that any minute now they would be crashing through the door looking for her.

"About being nominated for prom queen." Her mom sounded surprised. "Even Grace didn't tell me. It wasn't until Nancy Griffin across the street mentioned it to me that I found out."

"Oh, right." Mia tried to push the zombies to the back of her mind. "Yeah, go me."

"Well, I think it's wonderful." Her mom beamed, while somewhere in the background Grace slammed a knife onto her plate. Their mom turned around and lifted an eyebrow. "Honey, we've talked about this. You should be pleased that your sister is so popular."

"Pleased?" Grace scowled as she glanced over at Mia's outfit (skinny jeans, converse sneakers for running in case things got ugly, and her favorite David Boreanaz shirt for good luck). "How can I be pleased when she is making a mockery of a beautiful tradition?"

"Grace." This time their mom's voice was sharp, and Mia grinned.

"Don't worry, Grace. If I win, I'll make sure people know that we're related," she assured her, which only made her sister scowl even harder. Thankfully, before Grace could respond, Mia caught sight of Chase's Impala pulling up outside the house with Candice in the backseat. Oh, thank God. They were both alive. And in Candice's case, not looking like an extra from *Night of the Living Dead*. That had to be a good thing.

"Here's my ride." She darted over, gave her mom a kiss on the cheek, grabbed her bag, and raced outside.

"Hey," she said to them both as she slid into the front seat of the Impala. Chase was looking nice in a striped T-shirt, while Candice had obviously decided to go for zombie chic in a pair of ripped jeans and a pink hoodie with tiny vampires on it. "So are we all ready?"

"I've already eaten my body weight in pepperoni this morning. I'm way past ready," Candice declared. "So what's the drill?"

"Well, the senior assembly is in second period just after biology, so I was thinking I'd skip class and get everything set up, and you two join me when bio is over," he said. "The ritual is similar to the one you first did, but instead of using Algeria's crystals and amulet, we use cleansed ones. Then Mia just needs to chant the incantation but with the reversal spell added onto the end, and then it's all done."

"Good, and we can get back to the important business of getting ready for the prom. I swear I'm going to need a whole day at a detox spa to try and get all this protein out of my system," Candice said from the backseat as Chase made the short drive to Newbury High. He pulled into the parking lot, and just as they were getting out, he turned to Mia.

"Do you have your water? I think you're going to need it." He nodded toward the group of seniors that were gathering on the pavement, and Mia felt her stomach flip. She pulled a bottle out of her bag and gave herself a quick squirt and let out a sigh of relief as everyone started to wander away (not before mimicking her, though—had she mentioned how annoying that was becoming?).

They hurried along the hallway, and after checking for the third time that Chase had everything, Mia and Candice watched him slip into the gym, which was already being transformed for tomorrow night's prom. Several people on the prom committee were at the other end of the room fussing over a large glittery sign, but none of them even seemed to notice Chase as he headed for the bleachers. At first Mia thought that maybe they were purposely ignoring him, but then she realized it was just his way. After all, if she hadn't turned everyone into zombies and attracted his attention, she probably never would've noticed him, either. Which, in retrospect, would've been a pity since as it turned out, Chase Miller was a pretty nice guy.

Once he was safely under the bleachers, she and Candice made their way to biology. The bell hadn't rung yet but the class was almost full, and up at the front of the room Samantha was having an animated conversation with Mr. Haves.

"I just don't understand why you won't let me do a final run-through of my speech. Have I mentioned how important this is?"

"And yet I'm still convinced that it's best to actually learn about biology in a biology lesson," Mr. Haves said in a mild voice, seemingly unmoved by Samantha's plight. Ten points to Mr. Haves. "Now since you are on equipment duty this week, can you please go into the supply closet and get the microscopes? We're dissecting grasshoppers today."

"But who wants to find out more about grasshoppers or cockroaches that were dumb enough to get turned into brainless morons?" Samantha poked her bottom lip out and Mia gulped. *Yeah . . . wouldn't want that.*

Then she noticed the large ketchup stain on Mr. Haves's tie and the empty burger wrapper on the desk and she realized he must've been at the senior awards assembly, as well. Okay, she must not panic. Everything was going to be fine. Chase knew what he was doing and once they did the ritual, everything would return to normal. *Please let everything return to normal.*

She and Candice made their way to a lab table just as Samantha stalked to the supply closet at the back of the room, muttering as she went. Mia ignored her and sat down. Two seconds later, Rob walked in and made a beeline for her. She would've been a bit more flattered if it didn't look like he had just smelled a gourmet double-patty burger. She gave herself another light squirt of water.

"Hey, Mia." Rob yawned as he sat down next to her and gave her a sleepy grin.

"Are you okay?" she said in alarm, worried he had hit his stage-three zombie coma a bit early. "Maybe you need some Red Bull to help you stay awake. You definitely don't want to go to sleep. No way."

"Huh?" He looked at her blankly for a moment as his left arm started to twitch. "I'm fine. I just stayed up late last night trying to figure out my speech for today's assembly."

"Oh right." Mia felt a surge of relief flood through her. So no zombie coma, then. Well, that was good. "I wouldn't worry about it too much. I mean, everyone knows how great you are. You could probably just stand there and smile and people would vote for you."

"Or take off your shirt," Candice helpfully pointed out as she discreetly took a handful of Vitamin C supplements and passed them over to Rob. "By the way, take these. It will stop your arm shaking so much."

"They're not steroids, are they? My coach has given me strict instructions not to touch that junk."

"Definitely not," Candice assured him as they both watched him swallow the supplements. His arm immediately stopped twitching and Mia let her breath go. After her run-in with everyone in the parking lot yesterday, she just wanted to get through this class in one piece.

"Hey." Rob nodded at Candice. "Thanks for that—I feel

much better. Now I just need to figure out a great speech. You know, one that makes me sound smart or something."

"You mean like how it's your dream to erase carbon footprints or something?" Mia said, joking. Then she looked up in alarm as Rob scribbled it down.

"Thanks." He grinned. "I love dating smart girls."

Before Mia could say anything else, the bell rang and Mr. Haves stood up and started to take attendance.

Despite sitting next to Rob, Mia couldn't wait for the class to be over. It felt like an eternity, and by the time the bell rang her nerves were feeling pretty frayed. She jumped to her feet, eager to join Chase under the bleachers, but Candice seemed to be having problems getting her books back in her bag.

"Let me," Mia urged, but Candice waved her off.

"I'm not a brainless idiot yet," she insisted, and Mia took a deep breath and tried to be patient. Finally Candice got to her feet and they both headed for the door, but just as Mia was about to walk out, Samantha appeared at her side holding a large box filled with the microscopes they had just been using.

"Mia, do you have a minute?" Samantha asked as she fiddled with the top of the microscope.

"Why?" Mia narrowed her eyes in suspicion.

"Because I think I owe you an apology for yesterday," Samantha admitted.

"You know I'm not going to vote for you, right?" Mia double-checked, and Samantha nodded.

"Seriously, I just wanted to talk to you for a minute. Is that okay?"

"Fine." Mia let out a reluctant sigh. Candice was already farther up the hallway, but since her walking had slowed to a snail's pace, Mia figured she could just catch up to her. She followed Samantha back into the lab and folded her arms as the wannabe prom queen continued to collect the microscopes. "So what's this about?"

"I just wanted to say that after speaking to my mom last night, I realize I was a little bit hasty in blaming you just because people seem to like you."

"Well, that's very big of you." Mia shrugged as she looked at her watch. "And if that's all, I've got to go."

"Me, too." Samantha frowned as she picked up a couple more microscopes. "Actually, would you mind giving me a hand to put these away? I'm really nervous about my speech, and I think I need to run through it one more time."

"Well, I really need to—"

"Fine. Grace told me that you wouldn't want to accept an olive branch. I guess I should've listened to her."

"Oh, did she?" Mia bristled as she dumped her bag on the chair and grabbed the remaining microscopes before marching toward the supply closet at the back of the room. It was a huge walk-in closet with a security lock and steel doors, supposedly designed to guard against unauthorized access to expensive equipment and dangerous chemicals, but privately Mia thought it was more to keep out the smell of years of accidental spills. She wrinkled her nose as she flicked on the outside light switch and stepped in to put the microscopes on the shelf at the back. *Grace was just so freaking unbelievable, because—*

BANG!

"Hey!" she yelped in surprise as a loud noise went off from somewhere behind her, but as she spun around she realized it was just the closet door swinging shut. All this zombie business was making her far too jumpy. Soon she would become just as paranoid as Chase.

"Sorry about that," she started to call out as she twisted the handle. "I thought it was . . . Okay, so why can't I open this door?"

"That would be because I locked it," Samantha said in a cheerful voice from the other side just as there was a clicking noise and the space went pitch-black.

"You locked it?" Mia still didn't quite understand what was going on. "But why?"

"Because I'm about to give the most amazing speech ever, and I have no desire to have you try and overshadow me. You've already turned Rob against me—I'm not going to let you turn the whole senior class against me, too."

"Are you insane? You can't leave me locked in here." Mia used her shoulder to try and get the door to open. It didn't work.

"Of course I can. I did warn you not to take me on. That tiara is mine, and I'm not letting you get in my way. Oh, but don't worry. I've put some nice snacks in there for you—some leftover cupcakes and a Snickers bar—so make sure you don't forget to eat them."

If they were face-to-face, Mia would be staring at her in disbelief, but as it was she was left to stare into the darkness instead. She started to bang on the door again.

"Samantha Griffin, you let me out this instant. I know you don't believe me, but it's not about being prom queen—I just really need to get out of here. There's something important I need to do."

"I don't think so. The only important thing you need to do is learn your place, and since there is no class in here next period, I don't like your chances of getting out. Oh, well—see you at prom, loser."

Mia gave the door a couple more thumps but it was obvious by the silence that Samantha had left. She tried to glance around the closet, but since it was pitch-black, this was easier said than done. Had she mentioned that this sucked? Especially since, without her at the senior assembly to do the chanting, the reversal spell wouldn't work. And in turn she would be trapped in this closet until all the zombies came to eat her.

eleven

*F*ifteen minutes later, Mia's panic had turned into a full-blown breakdown. She closed her eyes and mentally tried to let Chase know where she was, but she had a feeling that her zombie-queen powers didn't exactly extend much past feeding the hordes of newly formed living dead. And, unless she got out of here quickly, that's exactly what would happen. Of course, the alternative was that Chase gassed everyone to death and that scenario left her feeling just as ill.

Mia gulped as she started to tug at the door handle again. *Think, Mia. Think.*

Perhaps she could dig a hole under the floor? Or through the wall? That might work. Ooh . . . or she could search the shelves and see if there was any equipment to explode the door. Of course the fact she didn't know how to really do this was a slight hindrance to that plan.

She was trying to decide which option was most feasible, when there was a ringing noise from deep in her pocket. For a moment she just stared blankly into the darkness before realizing it was her cell phone.

Okay, so calling someone was slightly more realistic than hole digging or creating an explosion and would have definitely been next on her list had she thought of it. She quickly yanked her cell phone out of her jeans and felt a huge surge of relief run through her when she saw it was Chase.

"Mia, where are you?" he said in a low, urgent voice. "The assembly has started, and I really think we need to do this soon, because stage three isn't far away."

"Samantha locked me in the supply closet after biology, and I can't get out. I don't know if it's because of the virus or because she just really wants to be prom queen, but either way, I'm stuck in here."

"Why didn't you call me?"

"I forgot I had my cell phone on me. Chase, I'm really freaked out. What if this doesn't work? What if we don't have enough time to do the reversal before the assembly ends? I mean, will they all go into their zombie nap and then—"

"Mia. Calm down. I'm on my way. We still have time but you need to relax. Take a deep breath."

"I can't believe you do this as your job." Mia took a deep breath and tried to gather her frayed nerves. "This is real. It's really, really real, and—"

"Okay, you might want to take a second deep breath," he added. "Right now, I'm in the biology lab and I'm on the other side of the door. You can put your phone away."

"You are?" Mia automatically shoved her cell phone back into her pocket and put her hand up to touch the heavy steel plate. On the other side she could hear Chase fiddling with the lock and her breathing started to return to normal. One more second and she would be—

"Er, Mia . . ." Chase called out from the other side.

"What? Please just open up the door. *Please, Chase.*" She felt her hand start to shake.

"I promise it's going to be okay. It's just that Samantha's used a padlock and a chain on this. Actually, I'm not even sure how she managed to lock it with her limited motor skills. Not to mention where she got it from. I'd have to say that she pre-planned it."

"Who cares how she did it, can you just undo it? Oh, and can you turn on the light?" The light instantly came on and Mia felt some of her panic subside. "Thank you. So what are we going to do?"

"Can you see any way out—a vent or an air duct? Anything?"

Mia looked around. "I see an air vent up above the top shelf."

"Okay. I need you to climb up, Mia. There is a vent outside this door and I'm sure they are both connected. If you can climb up there and through the shaft you can get back into the biology lab. It should only take a couple of minutes, and then we can go and do the reversal spell."

Mia's panic returned as she looked up at the ceiling, which

seemed to be about a hundred feet off the ground. "Okay, the thing is, we might have a bit of a problem." She gulped. On account of her fear of heights, there was absolutely no way in a million years she was going to be able to climb up there. She didn't care how many zombies might come along and try to eat her. She and heights were a bad match.

"What?" Chase said from the other side of the door. "Don't tell me the vent isn't there?"

"Oh, it's there all right." She inched as far away from it as possible. "It's just . . . I'm scared of heights."

"You're what?"

"I'm sorry, Chase. I can't climb up there, but I did have another idea of how to get out of here. How are you with explosives?"

She was pretty sure she heard Chase use a few choice swear words before finally saying, "Mia, don't move, I'm just going to get something to cut through the chain. I won't be long."

"Okay." She gulped, and what seemed like only moments later, she could hear Chase doing something on the other side of the heavy steel door.

"I've got a Bunsen burner, so I'll use it to burn through the chain," he told her. "The butane gas might smell, but it can't be helped."

"Thanks, and Chase, I'm sorry about the heights thing."

"We all have things that freak us out," he merely said, and Mia marveled at his patience.

"Still, it's really nice of you not to get pissed off. Especially considering this whole thing is my fault. It's because I'm too obsessive."

"What do you mean?" Even though she couldn't see him, she could almost picture his eyebrows rising up in curiosity.

"What sort of normal person goes and buys a love spell just because she doesn't want to get dumped before the prom?"

"Okay, so perhaps you're slightly obsessive, but no one's perfect. I worked on one case where I hid in a Starbucks restroom for three hours because I thought one of the employees was in stage two," he said.

"And were they?" Mia sniffed, holding her hands up to the door as if it might somehow help him.

"No."

She felt her mouth start to twitch with amusement, and she forced herself to clamp her lips together. "I shouldn't laugh, because sitting in a restroom for three hours is so not funny. In fact, if Candice were here, she'd probably tell you just how many diseases you could catch in there. Besides, I'm still more obsessive than you. I write lists of things I've done, just so I can cross them all off."

"I write lists and then destroy them in case they fall into the wrong hands," Chase informed her. "And if Rob wanted to go off with someone else, you should've just let him because it obviously means he's not the right guy for you."

"Shows how much you know about guys."

"You'd be surprised," Chase retorted, and Mia blushed despite the fact he couldn't see her.

"What I mean is that you're from the East Coast, so it's probably different over there."

"Trust me, testosterone is a universal thing," he said in a dry voice.

"Well, that might be right, but all I know is that guys like Rob don't normally want to date girls like me. In fact, *no* guys want to date girls like me. They all want a Grace or a Samantha." She sighed.

"So why do girls like you want to date guys like that anyway?"

"What?" Mia stared blankly at the door for a minute. "What does that mean?"

"Sorry, it's none of my business, but it just sounds like you said yes to Rob because he asked you, rather than because he was someone you really liked."

"Of course I didn't—" she started to protest, but before she could figure out just what it was that she did like about Rob, the door swung open to reveal Chase standing in front of her with a Bunsen burner in his left hand. Talk about a sight for sore eyes—and for one moment, Mia had the most ridiculous urge to hug him. After all, if it was Candice who had rescued her, she would've given her friend a hug. But then again, Chase wasn't exactly her friend—he was just the guy who had the crappy job of helping her fix the terrible mistake she had made. Helping her was just part of a day's work for him.

"Are you okay?" he checked.

"I'm fine." She collected her scattered emotions and stepped back into the biology lab as if she got locked in supply closets all the time. "So do we still have time to do this?"

"If we hurry. We're going to have to be careful getting back in the gym, though. Thankfully when I came out, Rob was just giving his speech about erasing carbon footprints. I'm not sure he knew what it meant, though, because he kept referring to keeping the sidewalks clean."

"Oh, no." Mia tried her best not to laugh. "Besides, he's very nice and sweet."

"So is my dog." Chase shrugged as they hurried down the hallway back toward the gym. They paused for a moment when they reached the double doors and peered in through the glass to where Samantha was up at the podium, passionately waving her arms in the air. Mia was just about to nudge the door open when someone at the back of the crowd turned and stared directly at her. A moment later, someone else did exactly the same thing, and then, before she knew it, the entire assembly had turned and was looking in her direction.

"W-what's going on?" Mia ducked and found herself instinctively clutching at Chase's arm.

"Crap," he muttered in a low voice. "I forgot to take into account that you're like a magnet for them—that's why they knew you were here. I guess the steel on the biology door stopped them from finding you in there."

Mia groaned. "Well, it's going to make chanting a little hard if they're all looking at me."

"Actually, I think that's the least of our problems," Chase said as Mr. Haves hurried over and opened the door.

"Samantha, your time is up," he shouted before turning and beaming at Mia. *Ew*, did he just try and sniff her arm? She realized that her water bottle was still in her bag, sitting on the bench in the biology lab. "Mia, there you are. Just in time for your speech."

"Actually, I'm not really sure about doing a speech," Mia tried to tell him, but the biology teacher didn't seem to hear her.

"Whatever you say, make it quick," Chase said in a low voice as Mr. Haves urged Mia forward onto the podium. "I'll be waiting for you behind the bleachers."

The minute she was up there, everyone jumped to their feet and started to cheer. She stepped up to the microphone as she caught sight of Chase and Candice, who were now in position and nodding for her to get there as soon as she could. She glanced at her watch. There was only another ten minutes before the assembly finished, which meant it was now or never. In the front row where the other nominees were sitting, Rob was giving her an encouraging smile and the thumbs-up sign.

"Don't be scared," he mouthed at her. "Just talk about that footprint thing. They'll eat it up."

Not exactly something she wanted to experience.

Mia gulped as she stood up at the podium and looked around her. Never in a million years did she think she would be standing up here. Never in three million years did she think she would be standing up here because she'd turned her entire class into mindless zombies. Who, she now noticed, seemed to be edging their way closer to the podium, their arms flailing at their sides and drool running down their faces.

Not good.

"Stop," Mia yelled out to them all, and was relieved when everyone came to a halt and looked up at her expectantly. "Look, I know you think you want to be near me, but really you don't. You've got to all try and think for yourselves. Do you hear me? Think for yourselves," she pleaded before jumping down off the stage and scrambling over to the bleachers where Candice and Chase were waiting for her. Behind her was the slow shuffle of feet, which let her know that they had kind of missed the point of her speech.

"God, that was so beautiful." Candice sniffed, and Mia looked at Chase in alarm.

"We need to do this now, don't we?" she whispered as she rubbed her brow and wished she had a do-over day. Actually two do-over days would be better, then not only would she not do the spell but she wouldn't say yes when Rob asked her out and she could simply go back to being the girl in Fringeland who was waiting for her life to get better once college started.

"Definitely," he agreed as he handed her the incantation. "You just need to do it exactly like you did the first time. Except at the end you need to read out the words I've added. That will reverse it. Okay?"

"Okay." She took a deep breath as she carefully stepped over the circle of sand into the middle where Chase had poured the mixture into the same wooden bowl they'd used last time. Her nose wrinkled in disgust. It smelled exactly the same, too. That had to be a good thing, right? All the same, she felt her hands start to shake, but as she looked into Chase's calm face, her terror faded.

She began to chant. By the time she got to the second page, her leg was tingling and the mixture swirled with smoke until finally she reached the end.

"Take away this curse. With this spell, I reverse," she called out before she opened her eyes and looked around her. The moment she got to her feet, Chase leaned over and helped her step out, his lean strong arms instantly reassuring as they clasped tight around her waist. She glanced around to where groups of seniors, who only minutes ago had been shuffling toward her, were now scratching their heads and looking confused.

"Did I tell you this assembly was finished?" Principal Keegan called out from somewhere behind them, and the seniors all spun around. "Because it's not. Get back here right now. We still need to discuss the ballots. I want them all handed in by the end of today. And don't forget classes end at lunchtime tomorrow so the prom committee can prepare for tomorrow night."

"So, do you think it's worked?" She watched as everyone

started to wander back to the main part of the gym, not even giving her a backward glance.

"I don't know." Chase studied the potion in the wooden bowl, which still had a faint swirl of steam hovering over it, before turning to where Candice was busy cleaning her teeth with a toothpick. "How do you feel?"

"How do I feel?" Candice finally put the toothpick away and looked up at them both. "I feel like I'll be sick if I ever look at another beef-jerky stick again. I swear I've eaten a hundred of them, and I have the most disgusting taste in my mouth. You know, I think I'd better call my doctor and see if I can get an emergency appointment to check my vital signs. What? Why are you both smiling like that?"

Mia turned to Chase and grinned. They had done it.

twelve

"So how does it feel to be a normal person again instead of a zombie queen?" Candice asked as they hurried down the hallway after the final bell rang.

"Well, I don't miss spraying myself with water ten times a day." Mia stopped at her locker to put her books in, pleased to see it was once again restored to its chaotic glory and there was absolutely no sign of zombie-queen-fattening food in it. As for how she felt, to be honest, the rest of the morning had been a bit of a blur. Chase had insisted on inspecting everyone's faces for any signs of the virus, but by lunchtime even he had been convinced. (Probably seeing Candice order a green salad had been the final piece of evidence he had needed.)

"I still can't believe I licked you. That is really gross." Candice shuddered. "Anyway, now that prom is officially back on, I'd better go to the mall and get my earrings. I decided to go for the silver in the end. Nothing like a near-death experience to help give a girl some clarity. Do you want to come with me?"

"I guess so. I still need to get shoes." Mia glanced around. "You haven't seen Chase anywhere, have you?"

"I passed him before I went into history and tried to thank him for saving me from a life of being a flesh-eating moron, but you know what he's like. He said you were the one who did it."

"Well, if he was left to his own devices, he would've gassed everyone," Mia pointed out as she walked through the front entrance and out in the afternoon sunshine. Funny how much brighter everything looked when you didn't think a zombie was about to jump out and eat you.

"He also rescued you from the closet, not to mention mixed the ingredients together," Candice reminded her as they walked toward her car. "Anyway, the important thing is that it all turned out so well. You must've been so relieved when Rob came up to you at lunchtime and spent the whole time talking about the corsage he's getting you."

"How can I be relieved when I haven't seen the corsage yet?" Mia wanted to know. "Especially since I have a very bad feeling he's going to get me a pink one despite the fact I've told him I hate pink."

"No, dummy. I mean, that he would still want to take you to the prom once the spell was reversed. You must've been really worried that you would be back to square one."

"Oh." Mia stared at her friend. Actually, she had been so busy worrying about trying to fix this thing that she hadn't had time to really think about what it might mean to her prom date. Still, the fact that Rob *had* sat with her meant he wasn't going to dump her. Perhaps this was what they meant by having your cake and eating it, too?

"Look, his ears must've been twitching." Candice turned to where Rob was jogging toward them with a broad smile on his face.

"Hey, Mia. There you are. Man, you're not going to believe this, but I can't get us a limo. I meant to order it during the week, but I totally forgot. So I was thinking of just grabbing a lift with Randy because the fender on my SUV is still all banged up. Are we cool if we just meet at the prom?"

"Oh." Mia flushed since it was probably because of the zombie virus that Rob had forgotten, so she couldn't really hold it against him too much. "Of course, that's fine."

"Great. You're the best." He grinned at her. "Anyway, a few of us are going down to the mall. Do you and Candice want to come?"

"Sure, we were going there anyway. I want to get some new shoes. Red shoes, *because I hate pink*," Mia said, in case he needed another hint about the corsage. At that moment, she caught sight of Chase hurrying down the stairs on his own. She waved at him and he slowed down as he reached them.

"Hey," he said as he thrust his hands into his pockets.

"Hey, buddy." Rob clapped him on the back. "We're in biology together. I hope I got your vote for prom king. Did you hear my speech? It was heartfelt, man."

"Of course he did," Mia assured him before turning to Chase. "So where have you been? I haven't seen you this afternoon."

He shrugged. "I've been around."

"Mia." Rob coughed. "We're going to motor—are you ready?"

"Oh." She turned back to Chase for a minute. "So do you want to come with us? We're all going to the mall—it could be fun," she said as she studied his face. It suddenly seemed like ages since she had seen him. For a moment, he returned her gaze and she felt her skin start to prickle, before he suddenly frowned and looked away.

"I can't. I'm sorry."

"Oh." She felt her face start to brighten in embarrassment as an awkward pause seemed to fill the space around them. "Right. I just thought . . . well, never mind. I guess I'll see you tomorrow morning, then."

"Yeah." He gave a vague shrug of his shoulders. "Anyway, you'd better not keep Rob waiting." He gave her one final look before striding toward his Impala. Mia watched him get into the car and drive away and tried to work out why it felt so weird. Probably because she really felt like they had shared something today. After all, they saved the whole senior class from turning into flesh-munchers. Then she frowned. He was a rule-abiding zombie slayer and she was the stupid girl who made his job harder, not to mention watched too much television and was dating someone who Chase thought was dumb. No wonder he couldn't wait to get away from her.

"Come on, Mia," Rob called out, and she realized he was already sitting in Randy's car waiting for her. She turned to Candice.

"I'll meet you there, okay?"

"Sure," her friend said as Mia hurried over and pulled open the door just as she caught sight of Samantha standing over by the stairs scowling. Well, at least some things never changed.

thirteen

"Wow, your mom is so cool. When I told my mom I was going to the prom, all she did was tell me not to buy anything in white because it would be a punch magnet," Candice said the next afternoon as they sat at the beauty salon having their hair curled and pulled in all directions.

"I know. It wasn't until I got home last night that she even told me that she'd arranged to have our hair and makeup done. Of course Grace was saying that she couldn't imagine not having a trial run first," Mia said as she flicked through the *TV Guide* and made a mental note to remind herself to TiVo a repeat episode of *Supernatural* that was on.

"As I've always said, Grace is an idiot." Candice muffled a yawn. "Man, I tell you—after everything that's happened, I swear I could sleep for a week."

"Well, you'd better have some more caffeine, because we've got a big night tonight."

"Yeah, that's what Chase said."

"Chase?" Mia turned to her friend in surprise before the hairdresser coughed and she was forced to face the mirror again. "I was looking for him everywhere this morning. Where did you see him?"

"I just bumped into him in the courtyard. He wanted to know what color my dress was," Candice said, and this time Mia really did spin around to face her.

"What?"

"Okay, so I didn't tell you in case you started harping on about the fact he is still upset about his dead girlfriend, but since I've got a spare prom ticket and he's had a tough week, I thought he might like to go to the prom—so I asked him."

"And?" Mia demanded in surprise.

"And he said yes," Candice said. "Stop looking at me like that."

"Looking at you like what?" she demanded as the hairdresser once again coughed and Mia reluctantly turned back to face the mirror. "I'm not looking like anything. I was just surprised, that's all—but if you're happy and he's happy then I'm—"

"Happy?" Candice guessed.

"Yes," Mia agreed. "Happy." Definitely. Of course she was. Why wouldn't she be? "So does this mean you're not going to get ready with me?"

"Don't be an idiot. Of course I'm getting ready with you. The thing is that since you're meeting Rob at the prom, I told

Chase to pick us both up from your place. So are you sure you don't mind?"

"Of course not," Mia assured her, which was perfectly true, because why should she mind? She was going to the prom with Rob. She had almost turned the entire senior year into zombies just so she could go to the prom with Rob. As for Candice—well, she deserved someone nice, and there was no denying that Chase Miller was nice. Very nice. And kind. Not to mention calm under pressure, caring, sweet, considerate.

"Well, if you say so," Candice said as the hairdresser stepped away and Mia was left to stare at her reflection in the mirror. Her shoulder-length brown hair had been smoothed down and coaxed into loose shiny curls and Mia, who had secretly been worried that she would end up looking like she'd put her finger in an electrical socket, couldn't help but smile at the end result. It was perfect. She turned to Candice, whose red hair had been clipped on the top of her head so it spiraled down in all directions. Then they grinned at each other and went through to get their makeup done.

"Girls, you look wonderful." Mia's mom clapped the minute they walked back through the door.

"Thanks Mrs. E," Candice said as she muffled another yawn. "It's awesome. Though seriously it felt like we were there for hours."

"We *were* there for hours," Mia clarified as she walked in

and her mom gave her a quick hug. "But it was totally worth it."

"Samantha has been working with Luanne, her stylist, for the last three weeks. Luanne is over there now supervising everything," Grace said, and Mia turned to see her sister sitting on the couch flicking through a magazine and looking annoyed.

"Whatever."

"Girls, it's prom night. No arguing."

"Fine. So Mia, tell me again what time Rob is picking you up?" Grace said.

Mia glared at her. "As I've already explained to you, I'm meeting him there."

"Oh, right. How could I forget?" Grace fluttered her lashes. If Mia hadn't just had her nails done, she would've been tempted to strangle her sister. As it was, she just ignored her.

"Girls, that's enough," their mom repeated. "Besides, if you're being picked up in an hour, you really need to go and get your dresses on. And don't forget I'm taking pictures."

Only an hour left? Mia yelped as she glanced at her watch, and the pair of them darted for the stairs. Once in the bedroom, Candice opened her bag and pulled out one of the cans of Red Bull that they'd bought on the way home.

"Do you want one?" Candice asked, but Mia shook her head. She was already too hyped, and she practically raced over to where her dress was carefully laid out on her bed. It really was happening. She was going to the prom. Mia Everett was going to the prom. With a date. Of course now that the spell had been reversed, she doubted she would be getting a close look at the prom-queen tiara, but that was hardly the point. The *point* was that—

"Candice, you probably shouldn't try and take that tag off while you're holding the can. You could spill it all over your dress," Mia said too late as she looked in horror to where her friend's dress was now covered in caffeinated soda, lying in a sodden mess on the floor. "Omigod. Your dress."

Candice seemed to be staring at the wet heap in surprise. "Somehow the can slipped. It's all over your carpet now. I'm really sorry, Mia."

"Don't worry about the carpet, worry about your dress! What are you going to do?" Mia picked up the delicate midnight-blue silk-shift dress that had totally suited her friend's red hair and stared at it in horror. "It's ruined."

"It's okay." Candice shrugged as she sat down on the bed.

"How can you not be freaking out about this?" Mia couldn't quite hide her disbelief.

"Remember that other blue one I tried on and I couldn't decide between them? Well, I ended up buying both of them," Candice said before shooting her a rueful grin.

"Oh, thank God you have a backup." Mia looked at her watch. "You'd better get going, then."

"Yeah, you're right." Candice got to her feet. "Hey, you don't suppose your mom will drive me home to get it, do you? It's just I feel a bit woozy—it's probably from all the caffeine."

Privately she thought it was more likely from the zillion vitamin pills her friend had swallowed during the day to counter-balance her "brush with un-death," but Mia kept her thoughts to herself. Instead she just gave Candice a hug.

"Of course she will," Mia assured her as they hurried down the stairs to explain what had happened. Once her mom and Candice had gone, Mia headed back to her bedroom and looked at her dress.

Up until now she had been too superstitious to take it out of the long, clear plastic bag it was covered in. And in retrospect, her superstitions had obviously been well founded. But now that everything was back under control, she had absolutely nothing to worry about, and she carefully peeled the plastic away from it.

She wasn't quite sure how long she stood there with a goofy look on her face before she realized she really should start getting ready, so she carefully slipped it on, the black silk rustling under her fingers.

She was just negotiating the ribbons that threaded across her exposed back when there was a knock on the door and her mom poked her head in.

"Need a hand?"

"Yes, please," she said in a grateful voice before glancing around. "Where's Candice?"

"Oh." Her mom carefully started to thread the ribbon through the eyelets at the back. "She said she was feeling a little tired and thought she'd take a quick shower to wake up."

"Man, I hope she doesn't get her hair or makeup wet," Mia said in horror as she thought how long they'd both spent at the salon. She'd purposely had a shower before she left to avoid such a challenge.

"I'm sure she'll be careful. Anyway, she said for you and Chase to go on without her and she'll just meet you there. Is she okay? She seemed to be acting a bit strangely."

"You could say it's been a strange week," Mia said, the understatement of the century. "Besides, you know what Candice is like. She's probably worried about her blood pressure or her red-cell count. She'll be fine."

"If you say so." Her mom gave a final tug on the ribbons and then stood back. "Now let's have a look at you."

Mia grinned as she slipped her feet into the cute red peep-toe shoes she had ended up finding yesterday. Perfect.

"Honey, you look gorgeous. And now if you're ready, it's time for some photos." Her mom beamed as Mia reached for her small purse and followed her downstairs to where Grace was standing in the hallway, peering out the small window at the side of the door.

"Oh, look, Samantha's date has arrived to pick her up. And that has to be the biggest limousine I've ever seen."

"Shut up, Gra—" Mia started to say, but the rest of her words were cut off as the doorbell rang. Before she could answer it, Grace darted toward it and pulled it open. Chase Miller was standing there holding a single red rose and wearing a hesitant smile on his face.

"Chase?" Mia said inanely. She pushed Grace out of the way and stared at him. "You're in a tuxedo. Y-you look really great." *Really, really great.* In fact, *so* great that Mia couldn't stop staring at the way his face had suddenly turned into a series of perfectly sculptured planes and angles. Or how the understated black jacket molded to his shoulders.

"So do you," he said.

"I do? Really?" Mia couldn't help but self-consciously touch the bodice of the black silk to check he wasn't teasing her.

"Yeah." He nodded before suddenly looking at the flower in his hand. "Oh, so I know you're going with Rob, but I figured since I was picking you up I'd better at least get you a flower."

"Oh, thanks." Mia stared at the perfect red bud while in the background Grace made a snorting noise before it sounded like she was being dragged off by their mom.

"I got one for Candice, as well. I hope she likes it," he added, and Mia felt herself come down to earth with a bump.

"Of course she will," she assured him while hoping that her cheeks hadn't gone red. "She'll be thrilled. Over the moon."

"Okay," he looked at her a little strangely. "Well, that's good."

"Yup, it's all good," Mia agreed a little bit too quickly. "So did Candice tell you that she's going to meet us there?"

"She sent me a text." He nodded, and Mia couldn't quite take her eyes off him. Had he always looked exactly like this? She honestly couldn't remember, because suddenly everything about him was so familiar yet so different all at once.

"S-so I guess we should get going," she stammered, still feeling completely flustered by the sight of him.

"Actually." Chase gave a polite cough as he peered over her shoulder. "Your mom looks like she wants to take some pictures."

"What? Oh." Mia spun around to where her mom was hovering in the background waving the digital camera and smiling. "Yeah, I forgot about that." She paused for a moment and nervously licked her lips. "Would you mind? It won't take long."

"Sure," he agreed in the same voice he used when he was helping her escape from the biology closet, and at just about every other step of the way before they did the reversal spell. It was obviously his "be polite to civilians" voice. Mia was going to miss it, and as Chase stepped toward her, the smell of his cologne invaded her nose so that she practically had to clutch at the doorframe for a moment. Her mom had obviously tied up the back of her dress a bit too tightly, she decided, as she led Chase in and started the introductions.

Twenty minutes later, her mom had finally finished the photographs and Chase was driving toward prom. Out of the corner of her eye, Mia studied his face, again marveling at how gorgeous he looked in his tuxedo. She loved the way he chewed on his bottom lip when he was concentrating. And the way his left hand tapped the steering wheel. In fact, the more she knew Chase, the more she seemed to be liking everything about him, and—

"So where are you meeting Rob, inside or out here?" Chase asked as he pulled into the Newbury High parking lot and brought the Impala to a halt. For a minute, Mia looked at him blankly before she figured out what he was saying.

Oh yes, she was going to the prom with Rob. Rob, who she had thought was the most amazing guy in the world, until in fact she had *met* the most amazing guy in the world and realized that Rob paled in comparison.

"Mia, are you sure you're okay?"

"What? Oh. Yes, I'm fine." Apart, of course, from being the biggest idiot that ever existed. But then Chase already knew that from the moment she had inadvertently done a zombie spell. And if he hadn't picked it up then, the fact that he had seen her *Buffy*-filled bedroom, found out she was scared of heights, and basically discovered that she was as shallow as he was serious would've hammered home the point.

"So?" he asked again. "Where are you meeting him?"

"Um, inside. Sh-should we go in?" she asked, and immediately regretted it as Chase reached out and touched her arm and a series of fireworks started to explode in the pit of her stomach. Final proof that she had fallen for Chase Miller. Talk about bad timing.

"I guess we might as well." Chase looked up at the front of the school that was now draped with fairy lights, as if that would somehow hide the concrete ugliness of it. The hallway was decorated in a mass of gold and silver balloons that led them into the gym. But when they reached the entrance, Mia stopped and stared.

It was almost impossible to decide what the theme was meant to be, but she had a feeling that if Tarzan ever wanted to open a nightclub, this is what it would look like: full of thick plastic jungle vines draped around the walls while silver disco balls and shimmering tinsel was hanging from every available surface, including the numerous white-clothed tables that were set up in the middle. Mia had no doubt that Samantha played a big part in choosing it all.

"Wow, it's really . . . ugly," Chase marveled as he held his hands up to his eyes to shade them from the brightness.

"Yup, welcome to senior prom." Mia frowned as she looked around. "By the way, where is everyone?"

"I'm not sure." They walked over to where a stage had been built. There were instruments and a microphone but no sign of any band members. Over at the far wall was a long table where the sodas and a large punch bowl were sitting. "Hang on, what's that noise?"

Mia looked over to where some screens had been set up (and subsequently draped in green vines and tinsel) and there was a large sign indicating it was where the photographer was. They walked over just as Rob and a couple of his friends wandered out from behind the screens doing a series of high fives.

"Mia, you made it. We've just been getting a few pictures taken." Rob came to a halt and grinned as the other jocks headed out to the main part of the gym. Over Rob's shoulder Mia could see there was a large group of cheerleaders and their dates still in with the photographer. So that answered that question of where everyone was.

"Oh, that's nice," she said, suddenly not quite sure how to answer him. Not that Rob seemed to notice as he continued to grin at her. He was dressed in a tuxedo with black satin on the lapels and pink cumberbund and bow tie. She couldn't help but think how much nicer Chase looked in his unadorned suit.

"So, I guess I'll go wait for Candice," Chase said in a low voice.

"Actually, I'm just going to go out to Randy's car and get Mia's corsage. You'll never guess what color it is?"

Mia looked at his cumberbund and sighed. "Pink?"

"Hey, yeah. I'll tell you, Chase, smart girls are the way to go. Anyway, I'll be right back," Rob said before ambling off in the direction of the door. Once he left, Mia noticed that the gym was slowly starting to fill up, and her nose twitched at the onslaught of perfumes all competing to outdo each other. Then she caught sight of Candice carefully making her way toward them wearing the second of the midnight-blue silk dresses.

"You got here. Are you feeling better?" Mia asked as she pushed one of Candice's curls off her face and noticed that her eyeliner was smudged. She knew the shower was a bad idea.

"I'll say." Candice nodded. "I actually feel great. I was

so tired and then I remembered that I'd bought these new multivitamin supplements. Anyway, a couple of them and a quick power nap and here I am, ready to go. Hey, Chase. You look hot."

"Er, thanks." Chase gave her an awkward smile and glanced around the place as if studying the spruced-up students. Then he looked at Mia and frowned. "Have you noticed anything weird?"

"What, like Samantha's dress?" Mia glanced over to where Samantha was currently holding court in a bright pink taffeta creation that looked like cotton candy.

"I'm not sure." He chewed on his full lower lip as if trying to figure it out, while next to her Candice jiggled her bracelets in excitement.

"Oh, I know what it is."

"You do?" They both turned to her.

"Sure, it's the food. Where is it? I can smell it, but I can't see it. How weird is that?"

"Smell it?" Mia frowned as she glanced around. "I can't smell anything but the perfume counter at Macy's."

"Really?" Candice looked at her in surprise as her nose continued to twitch. "Can you seriously not smell that? It's just like the most amazing thing ever. In fact, I'm starving."

"Candice." Chase suddenly asked in an urgent voice. "What does it smell like?"

"Why, chicken, of course," she said simply. *"Really, really great chicken."*

"Chicken?" Mia started to say. "I don't smell any . . . oh, crap." She took a step back and tried to stay calm. "Chase," she said in a low voice out of the corner of her mouth. "Did you hear that? What does this mean?"

"I'm not sure." He reached out and grabbed her hand and, okay, to be fair, she had been looking for an excuse to touch him, but this wasn't exactly what she'd had in mind. All the same she edged closer to him.

"What's wrong?" Candice looked at them both blankly as her right arm flew uncontrollably in the air. "Why are you both staring at me like that?"

"Candice, when you had that power nap before, how deep was your sleep?" Chase asked her, while his green eyes continued to scan the room. Mia tried desperately to read his face but it was almost impossible to do so.

"Man, it was amazing. I slept like the dead. Why?" Then Candice widened her eyes before clamping her hand down hard over her mouth in horror. "Are you saying the reversal didn't work?" Candice's voice was muffled as Chase continued to carefully study her face.

"I'm afraid so." He frowned. "It seems like whatever we did only slowed down the virus. But now it looks like it's active again."

"But that means—" Candice stared at him in horror.

"It means," Chase said in a dry voice, "that you're all going to turn back into zombies."

fourteen

"*B*ut how did this happen?" Candice moaned as she started to fan herself with her small sequined clutch purse. *Yes*, Mia would like to know the answer to that one as well, because they had fixed it. *They had.*

"I don't know." Chase led them over to a table in the far corner. "The department was concerned about us using a non-approved translation for the reversal spell, but since they didn't have the resources to help us do it in time, they let us proceed. But the important thing is not to panic."

"Not panic?" Mia and Candice both stared at him as they automatically followed him over and sat down.

"We've just had the week from hell, and now according to you it's going to happen all over again." Mia clutched at a piece of silver tinsel that was decorating the table as she tried to fight the nausea building in the pit of her stomach.

"Yeah." Candice agreed as her arm started to twitch in a jerky action. "Like *Groundhog Day of the Living Dead*."

"Look, I know you're both freaked out, but right now we need to just assess what's happening," Chase said in a calm voice that was belied by the numerous wrinkles in his forehead. He was worried, and if Chase was worried, it didn't bode well.

"Okay." Mia took a deep breath and tried to collect her thoughts. "So maybe there was a mistake in the translation?"

"Oh, so now this is my fault?" Candice widened her eyes in annoyance. "Because if we're going to point fingers, then let's not forget just why we were doing the stupid spell in the first place."

"You were the one who took me to visit a Chaos Maker," Mia retorted.

"Both of you, cut it out." Chase glared at them, his face pale and drawn. "This isn't helping."

"Sorry," Candice muttered. "I think it's all the residual protein that's left in my system. But the thing is, I didn't make a mistake in the translation. So why didn't it work?"

"That's the problem." Chase rubbed his chin. "It did work."

"Really?" Mia glanced over to where a group of hockey players were all licking their lips and waving at her. "Because I would beg to differ."

"Yes, but I checked and double-checked, and everyone was clear," Chase insisted.

"So?" Candice wrinkled her nose and Mia tried to ignore the fact that the skin around her mouth was starting to sag. "We did it right but missed something? Maybe I should've translated the rest of Algeria's notes at the end of the incantation?" she pondered.

"What?" Chase and Mia both stared at her before Chase finally spoke.

"There were extra notes? Why didn't you tell us?"

"Because you told me to just translate the ingredients," Candice protested. "And let's not forget that I had a virus that was trying to turn me into a mindless idiot. In fact, considering the circumstances, I think I did exceptionally well. I mean, how many mindless idiots do you know who could conjugate Latin verbs?"

"It's okay, it's not your fault," Mia assured her friend as she tried to hide her mounting panic. "And the important thing now is to translate the rest of the notes and redo the reversal spell. The book is back in my bedroom, so I guess we'd better go back there now. How much time do you think we have?"

"Not enough to get the book," Chase said in a flat voice.

"But I live only five minutes away," she protested before noticing that his green eyes were full of worry.

"Mia, this isn't like last time, when everyone was only in stage two of the virus. If Candice has already been in a coma, then it means they must be just about to hit stage four."

"Stage four?" Candice howled, and Mia winced as several people glanced over at them. Suddenly she wished the back of her dress wasn't so exposed because she got the distinct impression that her fellow students were counting her ribs.

"Right, so how about this. I call my mom and get her to

look in the book. Candice can tell her where the section is that needs to be translated and then we can go from there."

"Won't she think this is really weird?"

"I'll make up some excuse or something," Mia said.

"Well, what are you waiting for?" Candice demanded as she opened up her purse and pulled out a pen and paper.

"Wow, you're prepared." Mia raised an eyebrow.

"If I was prepared I would have my Latin books with me," Candice retorted as she impatiently tapped her pen against the white tablecloth. "Now call your mom already, Mia. I'm dying here."

"Okay, I'm doing it." She made the call and nervously looked around the room as she waited for her mom to answer. To an outside person, it looked like the start of a regular prom with groups of people standing and talking in awkward clusters, but it was only belied by the deadened expressions and the random arm twitching that seemed to going around the room. Finally the phone was answered.

"Hello? Mom, it's me," Mia said in a rush. "Look, I know this is going to sound weird, but—"

"Mia, everything that comes out of your mouth sounds weird," her sister's voice rang in her ear and Mia groaned.

"Grace, not now, can you put Mom on, please?"

"Er, that would be a no."

"Seriously, Grace, this is important." She looked over to where Chase was using his own cell phone to send a text message.

"I'm sure it is," Grace replied in a disinterested voice. "But Mom's at the grocery store and she left her cell phone here."

"What?" Mia yelped as Candice stared impatiently at her.

"You heard me. So whatever your emergency is, it will have to wait. Now if you don't mind—"

"Grace, stop!" Mia shouted as she realized her sister was about to hang up. "I need your help."

"Are you insane? Why do you need my help?"

"Because there is something I need you to do for me. Up in my bedroom there is a small black velvet book on the dresser."

"Oh, yeah, the one with Elvis on the front."

"What?" Mia was instantly distracted. "How many times have I told you not to go into my room?"

"I was only looking for my magazine," Grace argued. "Anyway, what was that book? It was all written in some weird language."

"Latin. The thing is, there is something in that book that I *really* need, so can you please go and get it for me? I've got Candice here—she'll tell you what page to look for, and once you've found it, you just need to read it all out to her. Okay?"

"What?" Grace demanded as it sounded like she was walking up the stairs. "Mia, you are at your prom and by some ridiculous freak accident you've even been nominated for prom queen, yet you want me to translate something in an Elvis book for you? What's going on?"

"Grace, please, it's a very long and complicated story and you probably won't even—"

But the rest of her words were cut off as Candice reached out and yanked the phone out of her hands with surprising strength (which didn't bode well if things got ugly).

"Grace, it's me. Mia turned everyone at the senior assembly into zombies and now we all want to eat her because she smells like the most amazing barbeque chicken that you could ever imagine. We want to eat Chase as well, but right now he still smells a bit undercooked. The point is that in the book is the answer of how to reverse this whole mess so unless you want the senior prom to end in a bloodbath and be canceled for future years, I suggest you do what your sister says."

Okay, so perhaps it wasn't so long and complicated, after all. Candice handed her back the phone, but there was only silence at the other end.

"Grace?" she called out. "Are you still there? I know it's a little hard to believe what Candice just told you, but—"

"Of course I believe you, Mia. It makes perfect sense. Rob has dumped you and you'd rather pretend that you've turned everyone into zombies than admit the truth."

Mia sighed. "Look, you can believe whatever you want, but right now I need your help. So if I hand you back to Candice, can you please tell her what it says?"

"Fine," Grace agreed.

"Really?" Mia couldn't hide her surprise.

"Yes, really," Grace said in a saccharine-sweet voice. "If you admit that Rob dumped you and has hooked up with Samantha, then I will help you."

"What?" Mia blinked before she realized her sister was serious.

"You heard me."

"Okay, fine." Mia gritted her teeth. "You were right. Rob dumped me and I was too embarrassed to admit it. I never should've tried to go against the laws of nature. Happy?"

"Of course not, because your actions could still have serious repercussions on my future social status," Grace retorted. "Furthermore, let this be a lesson to you to not do anything so stupid again, because—"

"Grace, please," Mia cut her sister off.

"Okay, geek-head. Don't get your panties in a twist. Put Candice on the phone so I can do whatever the stupid thing is she wants me to do."

"Thank you." Mia quickly handed the phone over before turning to Chase and shooting him an urgent look.

"Do you really think this is going to work?" she said in a low voice as Candice awkwardly held the phone up to her ear and started to scribble something down into her notebook.

"I don't know. I've just sent a message to my boss, and they are going to get a team out here as quickly as possible—but until they arrive, we're on our own."

"But even if we get the translation, what about all the ingredients?" she said, and Chase pulled a brown bottle out of his pocket along with the original incantation. *Oh, thank God.* Mia felt so relieved that she could've quite happily leaned over and kissed him.

"Got it." Candice looked up and handed Mia back the phone. "Now I just need to get this baby translated. By the way, do you think they have any food around here?"

Mia didn't like the way her friend was looking at her arm, but before she could comment, Samantha suddenly descended upon them in her horrible gown.

"Did you say 'food'?" the cheerleader demanded. "Because I'm starving. I mean, it seemed like a good idea to not do a sit-down dinner for the prom, because seriously most of the seniors at this school could afford to lose twenty pounds, but now I'm starting to regret that we didn't get the three-course menu. I swear I could eat about four cobb salads."

"Jeez, you know that those things are full of hidden cholesterol, don't you?" Candice blinked, and Mia tried not to notice that her skin was now tinged with gray. If her eyeball fell out or her skin ripped away from the bone, Mia could promise there would be some serious screaming.

"They are? Gross. Well, maybe I should just have some fingers instead and . . . *Did I just say I wanted to eat some fingers?*" Samantha turned to them in alarm and Candice shot her a sympathetic smile.

"Yes, you did. You see, we're turning into zombies and soon we're going to want to eat Mia and Chase," Candice explained matter-of-factly as salvia dribbled down her face. "But not yet. Apparently we have to wait until we hit stage four."

"Well, that's not fair." Samantha pouted. "First I can't eat any more cobb salads, and now I can't eat Mia Everett?"

"Of course you can't eat Mia Everett," Candice retorted in a disgusted voice. "You don't even like Mia. You tried to steal her prom date. Besides, I'm her best friend, so if anyone gets to eat her, it will be me."

"Um, Chase." Mia coughed. "I'm not sure I like the direction of this conversation."

"Okay, so how about this?" Samantha was telling Candice. "Do you remember that cute blue top I was wearing the other day? Well, if you let me have one of Mia's kidneys, I'll totally let you borrow it for a week."

"Make it a month and we've got a deal." Candice licked her lips and Mia gulped as Chase got to his feet and reached for her hand. Mia felt his fingers lace into hers, and she followed his gaze to where at least fifty seniors, all clad in their prom clothes, were laboriously walking toward them. *And was that Mr. Haves in there, as well?*

"I think we might have a problem," he stated unnecessarily.

"Is this the zombie-queen thing and they are going to start copying me again? Or maybe sniffing me?" Mia unconsciously inched closer to Chase. "Because this doesn't really look like last time."

"It's not like last time. Like I said, they are almost at stage four, which means we're running out of time."

Mia felt her knees start to buckle. Chase put a protective arm in front of her, and she found herself clutching at it for dear life.

"Oh, crap." Candice awkwardly got to her feet and shot

Mia an apologetic look. "Chase is right; stage four isn't too far away, because I've sort of got this overwhelming desire to eat you."

"How strong is this feeling?" Chase demanded.

"Oh, you know." Candice gulped. "It's pretty strong. Actually, Mia, I think you'd better run."

fifteen

*B*efore Mia could even answer, Chase grabbed her hand and dragged her along with him as he pushed through the students who were all closing in on them. "Let's go."

"But what about Candice?" She gasped as felt his fingers entwine in hers.

"I'm sorry, but we need to get you somewhere safe . . . quickly." Chase suddenly pivoted and started running in the other direction as a group of cheerleaders all wearing different-colored strapless dresses blocked their way.

Mia panted as she tried not to think about how terrified she was. The cheerleaders had now decided to run after them, along with everyone else, though thankfully they were moving at little more than a shuffle as Chase led her out through the side door that connected to the boys' locker room. Mia followed him and heard a crunching noise on the other side as the door swung shut.

The faint smell of chlorine and damp towels caught in her

nose as Chase continued to drag her along the tiled floor, past the rows of lockers. Behind them, the almost-zombies seemed to be having a bit of trouble trying to fit through the narrow door as they all tried to shuffle through at once. Mia dared to let out a sigh of relief that they really were a bit brain-dead. They hurried out through the other door with Chase stopping only long enough to kick a trash can to help slow the others down.

"Come on," Chase urged as they once again began to run. "We need to find somewhere to keep you safe."

"What about the school basement?" Mia panted, trying her best to keep up with his fast pace. Running in high heels certainly wasn't making it any easier.

"There is no basement," Chase said just as a group of tuxedo-clad chess-club geeks appeared at the top of the hallway. *And were they waving at her like this was a game?*

"What?" Mia yelped as they spun and headed left toward the library. "But there's always a basement. In *Buffy*, Sunnydale High has a basement bigger than a mall."

"I've studied the floor plans of this place enough to know that there is definitely no basement. Especially not a mall-sized one."

"Well, that's a flaw," she said, just as there was a shouting noise from behind them. Mia spun around to see Rob clumsily making his way toward them, closely followed by the others.

"Mia!" Rob yelled as he held out the limp and battered pink corsage. "Babe, stop with the running so I can hold you."

"In here." Chase pushed open the door of a janitor's closet and slammed it shut just as Rob's fist went crashing into the wood. Chase quickly locked the door and nodded for Mia to stand at the far end of the closet. She tried her best to look away from the small frosted-glass windowpane in the door that showed the shadowy dark silhouettes on the other side.

"Mia, come on. Let me in," Rob howled, and Mia felt a sense of doom go racing through her. This was it. She was going to get eaten. By her prom date.

Chase seemed to be searching around for something before he grabbed two brooms. He handed one to her before heading back to the door and pressing his full weight against it, as if to hold off what seemed like an impossible force on the other side.

"If anything comes near you I want you to belt them as hard as you can in the eyes, mouth, or groin."

Mia was just about to protest that she wasn't really the belting sort of girl, when all of a sudden she saw Chase's body shudder as someone kicked the door.

"So how long do we have before—"

"I'd say about an hour at the most." He face was grim as the door shook again. Oh, to be back in the steel-reinforced biology closet.

"An hour?" Mia clutched at the broom. "But that's not enough. How can we get it translated in time? Especially now that Candice isn't exactly on our side. Can we do just redo the old reversal spell? I mean, you've got it all there and it worked last time. Well, it did for a day. Maybe it would buy us some more time?"

"It's too risky. We got lucky then; this time it could backfire on us and make it worse."

"Worse than being eaten by two hundred zombies?"

"It could make them stronger. Even more aggressive. The thing is, without the translation, there is only one other alternative."

"Gas?" Mia's voice was faint as she noticed that Chase couldn't quite meet her gaze. Up until this moment the whole situation had all seemed a bit surreal, as if she had managed to wander onto the set of one of her favorite television shows, but now it struck her with blinding clarity just how serious it was. She really had turned everyone into zombies. Chase really was going to kill them all if he needed to, and if they both failed . . . well, then they really were going to be eaten.

"I'm sorry, Mia. But everything is already in place, since yesterday."

"What do you mean?" she said, the horror mounting.

"There is a hydrogen-cyanide device in the ceiling. All I need to do is remotely activate it with my cell phone, and it will release the chemicals that will kill everyone and stop them from turning into the living dead."

"What? Please, Chase. No. What about your department? Can't they translate it?" Mia was almost pleading now.

"How can we even get it to them in time, let alone explain—"

"Grace." She suddenly blinked as she reached into her tiny purse and dragged out her cell phone. "She knows the section Candice was talking about. I'll see if she can go online and try and Google a translation?"

"It's a long shot."

"A long shot is better than being turned into zombie kebabs," Mia retorted just as the sound of splintering glass shattered their ears. Chase immediately swung around and used the broom to hit away the hands that were trying to claw their way through.

Mia screamed as she saw Rob's face appear in the space where the window had been. Rob's hand went straight for Chase's neck and without thinking Mia ran over and used her broom to hit him on the knuckles. Rob didn't even flinch as he instead reached to try and grab her by the arm, but he was stopped by Chase's fist crashing into his picture-perfect face. Then, without wasting another moment, Chase dragged a free-standing locker over to cover up the exposed space where the glass pane in the door had once been.

"Okay." He leaned against the locker and panted. "I think you'd better make the call."

Mia didn't need to be told twice, and Grace answered on the third ring.

"Okay, so I've got a problem," she said without preamble and when her sister didn't interrupt she quickly continued. "You know that passage that you read to Candice? Well, we still need to get it translated. Like, right now."

"I thought Candice was doing that?"

"Um, yeah, there's been a change of plans." Mia shuddered as the banging noise increased.

"Oh man, don't tell me it's the zombies," her sister said, and Mia blinked.

"What? I thought you didn't believe me. You made me admit that Rob dumped me."

"I know, but that was before Samantha called me."

"She did?" Mia clutched at the cell phone. "What did she say? Are you okay?"

"Of course I'm not okay," Grace retorted. "Samantha was my role model and now she wants to eat my kidneys. But I can assure you that I have no intention of being zombie fodder. I've got the summer to look forward to and then it's my junior year, because—"

"Grace," Mia cut her off. "We don't have time for this."

"Oh, sorry. The only thing is, I'm not sure what I can do to help—"

But whatever Grace was going to say was lost as the locker started to shudder and shake with the force that was being thrown against it. Chase was using all his strength to push back, but it seemed as useless as trying to fight the tide.

"Mia." Chase used the chair to hit away a second hand. "I think you'd better wind it up."

"Grace, please just try. Go online and see if you can find a translation site. Anything," Mia pleaded. "And call me. We don't have much time left."

"Okay," her sister said simply, and hung up just as Chase grabbed Mia's hand and pulled her to him so that she could help him lean against the locker. At that moment she felt fingers reaching through from around the locker and trying to grab at her shoulder. She jumped away and swung at them, and from the other side someone made a howling noise.

"God." She moaned in despair as she rejoined Chase, leaning against the locker. "I've turned into a one-episode-only girl."

"What?" Chase panted as the door started to tremble, and he once again threw his weight behind it.

"Unlike some people around here, I don't spend my leisure time trying to kill things. I watch TV and everyone knows that the regular hero, aka you, never gets killed or, in this case, eaten. No, that sort of stuff happens to the one-episode-only girl. I'm dispensable. I'm the snack. While the likes of you move on to greater network success."

"Except of course this isn't TV," Chase pointed out as once again the door started to press open.

"No, and that's what makes it even worse." Mia waved her broom again as another hand tried to reach through. "I mean, if it were, then yes, technically I might only ever be known as the girl who was zombie bait in season five, but at least in real life I would still be alive, well paid, and—who knows—I might even end up as a cult figure who could go and do fan conventions. But there is no happy ending to this tale. I'm the loser of all the one-episode-only girls who ever existed."

The locker started to buckle and Chase seemed to use all of his strength to force it shut. "For a start, you definitely watch too much television, and more importantly, you're not going to die. Okay?"

"Chase, I want to believe you, but seriously I don't think the odds are stacked in our favor here, and—"

"Mia, stop it. I want you to take a deep breath and look into my eyes." Chase's voice was commanding, and Mia turned to him. His green eyes were still strained with the effort of keeping the almost-zombies out, but she nonetheless felt herself getting lost in them. Again. This was becoming habit-forming.

"Are you feeling calmer now?" he said in a soft voice, which made her oblivious to the door pounding that was resonating through her body.

"I . . . um . . . yes," she struggled to answer as she continued to stare deep into his gorgeous eyes. Would it be wrong to touch his face? She loved the way his jaw was tight with concentration. And how his full bottom lip was slightly protruding. How could anyone look that good? And—

Her phone started to ring and Mia reluctantly dragged her gaze away and saw it was Grace.

"Ingest it," her sister yelled into the phone as if she were speaking to an eighty-year-old who was hard of hearing. "They need to ingest it. That's why it didn't work properly last time. Oh, and by the way, I was talking to this totally hot guy on some zombie chatroom, and he said if you're stuck in a building with hordes of undead trying to chew your arms, the best thing to do is hit the fire alarm so the sprinklers come on. Apparently they hate water."

For a moment Mia just blinked before she finally managed to speak. "Thank you," she said inadequately. "You might have just saved us. But Grace, if you don't hear from me in half an hour, then things might've gone wrong and I want you and Mom to get in the car and drive straight to Grandma's house."

"Don't be ridiculous—you'll be seeing me in the morning, and I swear, if you get bitten by a zombie and have visible scarring, I will disown you," Grace said in a gruff voice, and Mia found herself sniffing.

"Okay, no visible scarring. I don't want your reputation to suffer," Mia promised. "But Grace, I mean it about going to Grandma's. Do you promise?"

"Yes, now go and do your zombie thing," her sister said in a softer voice. "And good luck." Mia finished the call and took a moment to compose herself before turning to Chase.

"Okay, so apparently under the blonde hair and short skirts my sister is a genius. The spell didn't work properly because the potion needs to be ingested. Oh, and she also suggested we turn on the sprinklers so we can get back to the gym."

Chase widened his eyes as he immediately reached for a mop that was propped up against the wall. "How did I not think of that?"

"It's probably because we were actually being chased by

real-life almost-zombies. It's very distracting," Mia comforted him before shooting him a hopeful look. "So what do you think? Can we redo the reversal spell *and* figure out a way to get everyone to ingest the potion?"

"Let's just take one thing at a time. First we need to get out of here, and then we can worry about the next part," he said as he pulled a small lighter out of his pocket and held it up to the mop head. "Now, when I say run, I want you to head straight for the gym. If something happens to me, you need to lock the door and do the ritual. Do you understand?"

Mia nodded as they waited for the mop to catch fire. Once it was blazing, Chase used his shoulder to inch the locker away from the broken windowpane. The instant he did so, hands and faces appeared from nowhere and Mia threw a bucketful of dirty mop water at them to buy him some time. That was all he needed, and he thrust his hand through the small gap and up to the ceiling, where he assured her there was a fire sprinkler.

Mia held her breath as they waited for something to happen. For a moment there was nothing, and then suddenly she heard a screaming noise. And another.

"Right." Chase now used his shoulder to shove the locker out of the way, and the pair of them glanced out the door to an almost empty hallway.

"What happened to them? Where did they go? Is this some sort of trick?"

"No trick. They've probably gone somewhere dry," he said

as he cautiously opened the door and Mia followed him out, holding her shoes in her hand since there was no way she could keep running in them. "Not all parts of the sprinkler system will have come on, just the ones that were triggered from the heat. But at least the coast is clear. For now."

"Let's do it then." Mia grabbed his hand and they ran back toward the gym through the misty water that was still falling down from the ceiling. The quickest way was to turn left, but the moment they did so, they caught sight of a group of students who had obviously been recovering from their impromptu shower. But the minute they saw Mia and Chase, they started lumbering toward them.

"This way." Chase nodded, and they slipped in through a classroom and ran through the adjoining door.

"Boy, you really did study those school plans well."

"In this business it always helps to know your escape routes. So how are you holding up?"

"Well, it's certainly not how I imagined prom night, but I'm okay. We just need to do this thing. And Chase, I'm sorry about your date. I guess this has pretty much ruined it for you."

"My date?"

"With Candice," Mia said as they made their way down the hallway.

"Candice and I aren't going on a date," he said in surprise. "Didn't she tell you?" He creased his brow together.

"Tell me what?"

He turned to her for a moment. "Because a reversal spell

has never been done before in stage two, when I reported it to the department, they were skeptical, because they had never approved the translation we used. Turns out they had good reason to worry. Anyway, they wanted me to continue to monitor it and since nearly all of them are going to be at the prom tonight, I had no choice but to go."

Mia frowned. "So where does Candice come into all of this?"

"She had a spare ticket. Yesterday afternoon I was at the school office trying to get one but they were all sold out. Anyway, Candice was up seeing the nurse and she overheard me. That's when she said I could have her other ticket."

"So let me get this straight, you're only going to the prom to make sure that the zombie virus really has been stopped and not because you and Candice are—"

"Definitely because of the zombies," he cut her off. "I mean, Candice is nice and everything, but this is strictly work, which she well knows. And why are you smiling?"

"I'm not smiling." Mia smiled. Chase didn't like Candice. He was only doing it because of the zombies. Then Mia put her hand over her mouth. Chase was dedicated to fighting zombies, and she was the shallow girl who not only created them but was standing there smiling in the middle of a crisis. Somehow she didn't think he would be changing his opinion of her anytime soon.

"Come on," Chase said as he opened a door that brought them back into the hallway. "We're almost there." They both stared at the gym door that was only feet from where they were standing, when a group of students suddenly appeared from around the corner.

"Look out!" Mia yelled as she dragged him toward the door, the sound of zombie shuffling not far behind them. She felt her lungs start to burst as she gasped for air before Chase finally put out a hand and pushed open the gym door.

Mia came to a halt as she cautiously looked around, but the place was deserted. Obviously the advantage of being the zombie queen was that even the lazy zombies had probably felt the pull to go out and find her. Of course, the downside of that was it wouldn't be long before they all came back.

Chase locked the door and hurried over to where she was putting her shoes back on. They were cute shoes. If she was going to be eaten, it was going to happen in style.

"Okay, so if you want to pour the potion into a bowl, I'll start chanting. But we still haven't figured out a way to get them to ingest it once it's done."

Chase glanced over at the punch cups. "I'm thinking that getting them to drink it will be the best shot."

Mia shot him a doubtful look. "I know I'm their queen, but won't they be too busy trying to rip my arms off to bother with taking a break to drink some punch?"

"If we do it before they hit stage four, it should work. Remember they like to follow your every move." Chase grabbed her hand and pressed the incantation sheets into it, then pulled a bag of sand from his pocket as well as the crystals and amulet. Then he kneeled and marked it all out again before taking hold of her hand and helping her step into the center of it. Mia gulped back her panic. *Should work* didn't exactly sound like great odds to her, and, *Hey . . . why was Chase Miller putting his arm around her waist?*

She looked back up at him in confusion as she heard a clicking noise but before she could make sense of what he was doing, he suddenly hurried over to the stage and picked up some sort of box that had a red button in the middle of it.

"Chase?" She blinked. "What's going on?"

"I'm sorry, Mia. It's for your own good," he said as he pressed the button and Mia felt a small tug around her waist.

"What's for my own good?" she said as she looked down and discovered there was a fat black belt tightly wrapped around her waist. Then she started to panic as a whirling noise started to come from somewhere. "Chase, I'm not sure I understand what—"

The rest of the words died on her lips as she felt her feet lift up off the ground. Her hands flew down to her waist to try and yank the belt off, but it wasn't going anywhere. She craned her neck and looked up toward the roof and her worst fears were confirmed. There was a thick piece of wire dangling down and it was connected to the back of her belt.

What on earth was a harness doing in the middle of prom? Then she realized that setting up a hydrogen-cyanide device wasn't the only thing that Chase had been doing yesterday afternoon. Mia started to scream.

sixteen

"Okay, so I know you're mad at me, but I promise I've only done it for your own good," Chase shouted out from below. "Besides, you were the one who told me to put the rule-book away and think outside the box."

"What?" Mia screeched as she tried to force herself not to look down. "This isn't thinking outside the box, this is a trip to Planet Insanity. Chase, I'm hanging in the air. With nothing to put my feet on. I'm well past being mad at you. I'm *furious*. Now get me down from here immediately, before I kill you. Or worse, throw up on you."

The harness started to swing and Mia felt sick.

How had Chase managed to do the one thing that scared her more than being eaten by zombies?

"Mia, I can't do that." Chase came back toward her and poured the potion into the punch bowl. Then he carefully threw an empty plastic cup up to her, which she found herself automatically catching. "Think about it, this is the safest way. You can do your chanting from up there and then when it works, everyone will see you pretend to have a drink. Simple."

Simple?

She threw the cup back at his head. However, on account of being too scared to open both her eyes, it missed him and bounced harmlessly onto the floor on the other side of the table.

"Please, Mia, I'm trying to help you."

"Help me?" Mia tried to see if there was another punch cup she could throw at him, which in turn caused the harness to jiggle and she felt herself sway in the air. "Did you miss the little conversation where I told you I hated heights?"

"That's why I didn't tell you what I had planned. I didn't want you to worry."

"Well, it didn't work," she yelled at him. "Because see this? This is my worried face."

"Mia, please, can we talk about this later? You need to start doing the incantation because we're running out of time." As he spoke, he pointed over to the locked door, which, from the sounds of the fists that were hammering it, wouldn't be locked for long. Then he shot her a pleading look. "It's the only way I can keep you safe."

Mia couldn't believe this was happening. She hated heights. She hated Chase for making her be up here. And while she was at it, she also hated—

"Zombies!" Chase yelled up to her. *Yeah, she really hated zombies as well. . . .*

Then she realized Chase was pointing to the gym door, and Mia turned her neck as far as she dared. Mind you, when she caught sight of ten students lumbering in, she almost wished she hadn't. Their eyes were vacant, there was a lot of drool going on, and most disturbing of all, their mouths looked a lot bigger than they had before. Somewhere in the distance a figurative dinner bell was obviously sounding, and Mia let out a long groan. It looked like stage four was rearing its ugly head.

Chase darted back toward her, and for one blissful moment, she thought he was going to lower her down—but instead he picked up the broom he had brought with him and held it up.

"Mia. You've got to start chanting. Right now!"

She started to read the words. The other two times she had done it, she had sort of drifted off into a dream. But now, all she could feel was terror. She dared to peer down and saw Chase punching Principal Keegan in the face.

"Any good news for me?" he yelled.

"I'm sorry, I don't think it worked. I'll try again," she said as she moved slightly and then felt herself sway in the air. The motion made her ears throb and she took a deep breath before commanding herself not to faint.

"Just remember you need to focus."

"Yes, well, perhaps it wouldn't be so hard if I wasn't dangling up in midair," she snapped. *Or if there weren't quite so many almost-zombies down below her in the gym.*

Chase had now jumped up onto a stack of chairs and was

trying to kick away a couple of seniors. "Anytime now would be great," he said through gritted teeth.

Okay. She could do this. Mia took a deep breath and started to chant again. *But why was it so noisy down there? And this black belt was really starting to chafe at her skin. Perhaps Candice would know some good cream to put on it—*

"Mia." Chase's voice boomed in her head. "We don't have long. And then—"

"Then what?" She gulped and, despite hanging in the air, she couldn't help but notice the determined gleam in his green eyes.

"I have to release the gas."

Mia felt sick with horror. She didn't want to be eaten, but being gassed to death was definitely next on her list of how she never wanted to spend her prom night. Or any night, come to think of it. She used the incantation to fan herself.

"If this reversal spell doesn't work, then everyone here is going to start trying to eat you . . . very soon. Trust me, my way is a lot more humane."

"It's also pretty final." She could feel tears of panic welling up in her eyes, and her voice wobbled as once again the full enormity of the situation hit her like a rock on the head.

There was only one thing to do. She was going to chant loudly. However, once again, by the time she finished, the punch bowl down on the table didn't look remotely steamy.

"Chase," she cried. "It's no good. I'm so sorry. This was the worst idea ever. And it's all my fault. I've never had a good attention span, and if only I hadn't tried to be so controlling. I mean, so what if Rob had dumped me? I should've just let it happen instead of trying to . . . Chase . . . *where are you?*"

"I'm over here," he yelled, and she swiveled around, this time not even noticing how much she was now rocking in the air. All she could see was that Chase was cornered by about a dozen zombies and one of them had Chase's arm in their mouth and—

"*No!*" Mia screamed at the top of her voice and the whole gym went quiet. Then without even looking at the paper again, she began to chant. Over and over she said the words. Over and over she refused to let the image of Chase being used as a zombie snack take hold in her mind.

Finally, after what seemed like hours—but was probably only a couple of minutes—she felt her leg tingle, and she looked down at the punch bowl, where the potion now had wisps of smoke rising up from it.

"It worked." She blinked as she looked around. "I did it. It worked. It felt exactly like it did the first time. Oh my God. I did it."

"Mia." Chase's voice sounded faint as he lashed out at everyone who was trying to attack him. "That's not enough. Remember, you need to pretend you're drinking from a cup, so that they can all copy you."

"Oh." Mia felt her face go pale. "I guess it probably wasn't such a good idea to throw it at you before then."

Well, she hadn't come this far to have it all fall to pieces now. She was just going to have to improvise. While hanging from the ceiling. No pressure then.

"Drink," she called out to them all. "I'm your queen and I say you should drink."

"Drink your blood maybe," someone heckled and suddenly what seemed like a million eyes all turned upward to where Mia was still dangling in the air. Hmmmm. That probably wasn't such a good idea. She cupped her hands into the shape of a small bowl and held them up to her lips.

"Boy, this punch is good stuff. Really delicious."

Chase, who had managed to wriggle free during the distraction, made a groaning noise and if she wasn't mistaken he was rolling his eyes. Hey, at least she was trying.

"Yum," she hollered, as they stood rooted to the spot, still staring at her. She pretended to gulp some more from her imaginary cup. "Don't you all want to get yourself a nice lovely drink? Anyone? Hey." Mia suddenly felt herself sway in the air again and an uneasy feeling lodged itself in her stomach as she glanced over to the harness controls.

They were now in Mr. Haves's hands. She was fairly certain that it wasn't ethical for a biology teacher to feast on the bones of any of his students, but the way his eyes were gleaming at her, she had a feeling that *zombies* and *ethics* weren't two words that were often heard together. Unfortunately.

"Chase," she yelled, but it was no good. He was being held over at the far wall and even she could tell it would be virtually impossible for him to get to her in time.

"What's wrong, Mia?" Mr. Haves yelled out to her as she felt herself slowly being lowered to the ground. She tried to ignore the way the saliva was dribbling down his face. If he thought she was going to say nice things about him in her teacher-evaluation form, he had another think coming. She felt herself start to wobble as the harness continued to get closer to the almost-zombie crowd who were eagerly waiting for her with outstretched arms.

Mia lifted up her legs so no one could grab at her ankles and for a moment wished she hadn't worn heels, because they were making her a good two inches closer to the hordes of hungry—

Heels.

That was it! And before she could even remind herself of just how expensive her adorable peeptoe shoes had been, she stretched out and ripped one from her left foot. Then she forced herself to open both eyes, take aim, and throw it as hard as she could at Mr. Haves's head.

"Not so fast," she yelled as it hit him right in the middle of the forehead. For a minute he looked a bit stunned as he rubbed the red mark on his forehead, and then he started to laugh.

"You know that didn't hurt, right?" He grinned and revealed his wide mouth. "And furthermore . . . *Ouch.*"

This time he really did look stunned as a second shoe hit

him in the head. Mia blinked, since it hadn't occurred to her
to try again, and this time the culprit appeared to be a tat-
tered-looking Vans sneaker.

"Hey, stop it," he yelled as a third and a fourth shoe all
went flying in his direction. Mia swiveled her head and realized that everyone below her was now reaching for their shoes
and throwing them directly at Mr. Haves's head.

Oh, great. So they have no problems copying her when it
came to shoes, but they wouldn't drink a lousy glass of punch?

Still, at least she had the consolation of seeing Mr. Haves
fall in a heap to the ground. But her happiness was short-lived
as Rob picked up the controls and started to fiddle with the
buttons.

"No," Mia yelled at him. "You so don't want to do that.
Why don't you have a nice glass of punch instead? Drink.
What a great idea. Go on, you know you want to," she urged
them as once again she cupped her hands and held them up
to her mouth. But it was no good, and the only response she
got was that a few of those closest to her started to lick their
lips.

Rob grinned as he pressed a button and once again Mia felt
the harness lowering her slowly down to the waiting crowd.

She was so totally screwed that it wasn't even funny, and
for the first time in her life, she wished that she could stay
higher up in the air. As it slowly lowered down, she caught
sight of Candice laboriously trudging across the room, her red

hair wild and frizzy from the fire sprinklers and her makeup running all the way down her cheeks.

"Candice," Mia shouted, and was relieved when her friend looked up to the ceiling. Of course it would help if she was looking in the right direction. "Turn around, I'm over here."

However, Candice continued to just look blankly the other way. Whatever Candice's ridiculous health ritual had done to slow down the virus had obviously stopped working. Then she realized her friend had probably been too brain-dead to remember to take whatever her latest supplements were.

"Candice, open your purse, get out your vitamins, and swallow as many of them as you can."

For a minute she didn't think her friend had heard, but finally she unzipped her purse and pulled out a large white jar. Her hands shook as she tried to get the lid off, but eventually she managed it and Mia watched in amazement as Candice swallowed pill after pill in what had to be some sort of Olympic medal display.

Mia was so engrossed that she hardly realized the harness was slipping closer to the ground until she felt fingers tightening around her ankle. "Candice, please, you've got to get them to drink the potion. It's in the punch bowl," Mia yelled as she tried to kick the hands away.

"Hey, you dumb-ass zombies," Candice suddenly yelled, her mouth still smeared with the remains of what looked like Vitamin C supplements. "If your queen tells you to do something, you do it. Now drink the punch."

"But why can't we just eat her first and then have a drink?" someone demanded, and Candice spun around and raised a straggly eyebrow at the dissenter.

"I'm sorry but am I hearing things?" Candice demanded as she picked up a chair and threw it at the person. Then she turned back around, dusted her hands on her slightly worse for wear midnight-blue dress and held her glass into the air. "Now, I'm going to have some of this fine punch. Cheers, Mia."

For a moment there was silence before another student shuffled forward and started to drink. "Hey." He nodded at Candice in approval. "This stuff is pretty good."

"And apparently it has no calories in it," Samantha added as she awkwardly tottered over to the bowl and followed suit.

For a moment Mia watched in stunned amazement as one by one everyone drank the reversal potion. In fact, they were all rushing toward the table, determined not to miss out.

"That's it, buddy." Candice handed a cup to the next person in the line. "No, don't try and lick my hand, just finish drinking."

"Candice," Mia called down. "Do you feel any . . . *different?*"

"Well, I still think I might have leprosy, but I'm pretty certain that the *Viral Zombaticus* has left the building." Her friend looked up and grinned, and Mia let out a huge sigh of relief as she saw that Candice's skin was now only covered with smeared makeup and not zombie drool. "Which means you managed to do the spell. Yay, you."

"Yay, all of us," Mia amended with a grin as she caught sight of Chase over on the stage holding up the controls to let her know he was going to lower her down. It had worked. They had really done it.

seventeen

"And now Mia, I want you to repeat after me. There was a fire, you inhaled some smoke. It made you feel a bit . . . strange. But everything is back to normal now."

"No, we lit the fire to turn on the sprinklers so we could run away from the zombies." Mia folded her arms and wondered just how long she was going to have to sit out in the hallway listening to this guy try and convince her that what happened didn't happen. She glanced at her watch. It had been half an hour since the spell had been reversed, and in that time, the place had been swarmed by firefighters and at least thirty of Chase's Department of Paranormal Containment colleagues. Including this monkey.

"No," the guy repeated in a firm voice. "No zombies. Zombies don't exist. It was a fire."

"Zombies." She glared back at him.

"Fire." The guy gritted his teeth. "It was a—"

"It's okay, Jon, I've cleared it. You don't need to keep trying to do the memory adjustment," a voice said, and Mia looked up in delight to see Chase standing just feet away from them. Her heart started to flutter.

This was the first time she'd seen him since he let her out of the harness, and even when she'd run over to thank him, he'd been whisked away by someone else. Still, he was here now and looking far more glamorous than anyone had a right to considering what they'd just been through. Even the smudge down the right-hand side of his cheek looked debonair.

"Thank God." The guy got to his feet and wiped his brow. "I've debriefed thousands of survivors before, but I've never met such a stubborn mind."

"Not stubborn—clever," Chase corrected as he narrowed his eyes and glared at the guy. "She's the first person to ever manage a stage four reversal spell, so watch it."

"That was her? She's the queen who survived?" Jon suddenly looked at her with newfound respect, which would be nice if Mia knew quite why he was doing it. "I didn't realize."

"Yeah, well, now you do. Anyway, the boss wants you back in the gym. They've dismantled the hydrogen-cyanide device, and there are only five more people to be debriefed, so once that's done you're clearing out."

"What about you? Are you coming?" Jon asked as he headed back to the gym doors, but Chase shook his head.

"No. I've still got my senior prom to go to."

"Prom's still on?" Mia waited until Jon had disappeared before getting to her feet and racing over to where Chase was standing, his thumbs looped through the waist of his tuxedo pants, looking awkward.

"They figured it would be best to do it like that to help ensure that no one remembers," he said, not quite meeting her gaze. "Speaking of which, it looks like Jon had quite a struggle trying to get you to forget."

"What can I say?" She shrugged. "I guess I just believe different things than other people."

"Thankfully you're the only one. The debriefs have been one hundred percent successful apart from you. The reason it didn't work is probably the same reason you could still remember where you bought the spell from in the first place," Chase said, still not looking directly at her, and Mia felt some of her excitement start to fade.

"What's wrong? Is everything okay? Is there something you're not telling me?" She tried to study his face for clues, but he wasn't giving anything away.

"Everything's fine." He ran a hand through his short hair. "Anyway, I'd better get back. I still need to give a final report to my boss, but I just wanted to check that you were okay."

Well, she had been until he had started acting all distant on her again. And after everything they'd been through. But, before she could say anything, Candice came racing toward her and Chase quietly slipped out of sight.

"There you are," Candice said. "I've been looking everywhere for you. We've got to get back in there, because the band has just shown up and they're about to announce the prom queen and king." Her friend dragged Mia to the gym, where everyone was standing around looking completely normal (apart from being slightly wet).

"Oh, right." Mia blinked at her friend in surprise. "With everything that's happened I kind of forgot about that."

"Mia Everett, you have defied the odds and been nominated for prom queen and now you're telling me that you forgot about it? Are you feeling okay?"

"Um." Mia rubbed her brow in confusion. This ending definitely wasn't like anything she had seen on *Buffy* before. First up, Chase was meant to be happy to see her, but instead he seemed determined to avoid her at all costs, and now Candice, her best friend, appeared to have no memory of anything that had happened.

"I knew it! You're not feeling well, are you?" Candice looked concerned. "You know, I've always thought you had a bit of recurring mono. I bet that's it."

"No." Mia shook her head. "Honestly, I'm fine. I just inhaled too much smoke from the fire."

"True." Candice nodded her head before pausing for a moment. "Of course another, more likely reason is because of all the zombies you've just spent the last hour fighting."

"You remember?" Mia accused, and Candice just shrugged as she pushed through the crowd so they could get closer to the front.

"Of course. I mean, how stupid do they think we are to fall for those amateur memory-readjustment techniques? Not that

I told them that. The guy who was debriefing me was very cute so it was nice to have an excuse to stare into his eyes."

"Candice Bailey, you were trying to hit on the guy who was debriefing you?" Mia turned to her friend in surprise.

"What, it's all right for you to do it but not me?" Candice demanded as she ignored the dirty looks people were giving her for pushing in.

"Jon? Trust me, I wasn't hitting on him." Mia rolled her eyes. "He was an idiot, and—"

"No, not that guy. I mean Chase."

"Oh." She blushed as she recalled that Candice had actually asked Chase to the prom as her date. "Of course I don't like Chase," she protested. "That is crazy talk. How could I like someone that you like?"

"Me? Who said I liked him?"

"You did," Mia reminded her. "On numerous occasions."

"Yes, but only so that I could get you to admit that you liked him," Candice explained in a patient voice, and Mia felt her mouth drop open.

"But why would you think that? I never once said I liked him. I didn't even think he was cute."

"I rest my case." Candice grinned. "Since the fact is he is very cute and if you didn't like him, then you would've been quite happy to acknowledge this."

"Okay, fine." Mia threw up her hands in defeat. "But it doesn't matter anyway, because now that the crisis is over, he couldn't get away from me fast enough. You know, I'm sick of living in the real world. I think I'm going to stick with television from now on. It's a lot less draining."

"And here I was thinking that you were clever." Candice rolled her eyes. "The only reason he was being funny with you is because you seem to have forgotten that you've already got a date for the prom. In fact, you almost turned the whole senior class into you-know-whats just so you could go to the prom with this particular person. And Chase is many things, but I doubt he's a mind reader."

Mia widened her eyes. "You mean, you think he—"

"Well, duh." Candice shot her a sympathetic look as if to say she was pleased Mia had finally caught up.

"I've got to find him." Mia started to glance around her, desperately looking for a tall zombie hunter with short light brown hair and the sort of green eyes that a girl could get lost in. "Where is he—"

"Shhhhh," someone from behind them hissed. "They're about to announce the winners. And hey, aren't you supposed to be onstage with the rest of them?"

Mia blinked for a moment before realizing that Rob, Samantha, and all the other nominees were all lined up at the back of the stage looking exactly like they belonged there.

"Crap." Candice scowled as she tried to push Mia around the stage so she could climb up the stairs. "I knew I forgot something."

"Don't worry about it." Mia shrugged just as Mr. Haves

stepped up to the podium with a large bandage wrapped around his head. Mia sent him a mental apology since she had a feeling one of the marks would probably match the heel of her shoe.

"And it gives me great pleasure to announce that Newbury High's prom king is Rob Ziggerman." Around them people started to whistle and clap as Rob got up to the podium and gave them all a goofy grin. Mia sighed. There was no denying that Rob was very good-looking, but the problem was that there was no real substance to him. What you saw was what you got. Unlike Chase, who seemed to have more layers than an onion.

Rob gave the crowd a wave as he readjusted his crown to no doubt make sure it didn't ruin his hair. In the background Samantha was smoothing down her gown in anticipation as Mr. Haves headed back to the microphone.

At that moment Mia caught sight of a familiar figure just to the left of the stage. *Ah, there he was.* For a moment she just stared at him. He was so perfect. So kind. So clever. And okay, yes, he was incredibly good-looking as well and the sooner she got over there and—

"And the prom queen is . . . Mia Everett," Mr. Haves called out.

"What?" Samantha howled from the back of the stage, only sounding slightly more surprised than Mia herself, who had been busy looking at Chase.

"So, is Mia Everett here?" Mr. Haves turned to the other girls on the stage before frowning. "I'm not sure that Mia is here. A couple of our students had to go to the hospital due to mild smoke inhalation from the fire we had earlier, so—"

"Not so fast, she's right here," Candice yelled out before grabbing hold of Mia's hand. "Out of the way—prom queen coming through," she snapped to the people standing by the stage steps and then with a final push, she guided Mia in the direction of the stage.

"Well done, Mia." Mr. Haves gave her a smile as someone else thrust a tiara on her head and a sash around her shoulders. Then before she knew it, she was standing next to Rob under the spotlight. She spun around to try and find Chase, but he had disappeared. So much for her big chance to explain to him how she really felt. She was just about to go and look for him when Rob grabbed her hand.

"Hey Mia, congratulations. I can't think of anyone who deserved prom queen more."

"I don't think Samantha would agree with you," she said in a dull voice as she glanced over to where Samantha was having an animated conversation with Principal Keegan (no doubt lodging her formal protest). "Anyway, congratulations to you, too. So what happens now? Are we supposed to dance or something?"

"Yeah. Look, don't take this the wrong way, but would you mind if we skipped with tradition? I've got a headache. Actually, it feels like I've done five rounds with Muhammad

Ali. Must've been from the fire. Anyway, I think I might need to get it looked at."

"Oh, right." She flushed. "Sure."

"Plus." He suddenly grinned at her. "I think if I danced with you, that guy from our biology class who is standing behind us might just kill me. He doesn't say much, but I the get the feeling he could handle himself in a fight, and I don't want to take any chances."

But Mia hardly heard him as she spun around to see Chase leaning against the wall with a small smile tugging at his full bottom lip as his green eyes caught hers.

"I thought you'd left," she croaked as he started to walk toward her, his eyes never leaving hers.

"I almost did," he admitted. "Because the idea of watching you and Rob together wasn't exactly high up on my list of fun things to do."

"I know, but Chase . . . about Rob . . . I was such an idiot. I mean, he's a nice guy, but he's not the guy for me."

"Really?" He stopped just inches from her and seemed to be studying her face.

"Really." She nodded and smiled. "You see, this really amazing guy I know once told me he thought I said yes to Rob just because he asked me, rather than because he was someone I really liked."

"Sounds like a smart guy," Chase said as he took another step toward her.

"He is," Mia agreed. Somewhere in the background the

music had started to play but she wasn't conscious of anything but Chase. "Very smart."

"Mia, about the harness." He suddenly frowned. "I'm really sorry. I should never have done that, but after what happened to Audrey, I just couldn't bear the idea of you getting hurt."

"Really?" she croaked. "But I don't understand. I've made so many stupid mistakes. And I watch way too much TV. How can you like me?"

"I tried to gas the whole senior class. And I pay way too much attention to the rulebook. How can *you* like *me*?" he countered as he finally closed the distance between them and snaked his arms around her waist. His face was just inches from hers and she caught her breath. He was like no one she had ever met before, and she was fairly certain that if he wasn't in her life every single day, she would be very sad indeed.

"P-perhaps we could just call it even?" she suggested in a flirty voice as her heart started to pound like a drum in her chest.

"'Even' works for me," he rasped as he lowered his head even closer to hers. "But there's something I've got to ask you."

"What?" she said as his hands tightened around her waist and she felt her knees start to buckle.

"Do you think we could stop talking now so I could kiss you? I've heard that it's how all the very best TV shows end."

A smile tugged at her lips, and Mia felt the most glorious rush of joy go racing through her body, but before she could even answer, Chase's mouth came crashing down on hers. She shivered in delight at the feel of his lips on hers, and in turn he deepened the kiss. His cheek rubbed against hers as she melted into his chest and snaked her arms around him, because the feel of Chase so close to her made her feel . . . like a queen.